MW00945030

Rekindled

Hillary Craig

ISBN: 1490573674
ISBN-13: 978-1490573670

For Andrew. I couldn't have done this without you. You've always believed in me and I can't thank you enough for that. I love you!

Acknowledgments

Special thanks to all of my family and friends for all of their love and support throughout this process. I'd also like to thank Lisa Greenberg and Matt Sumpter for all of their guidance and help.

Priya,
Thank you for being an amazing friend! I hope you can enjoy reading this at the beach.

Love,
Hillary

Chapter 1

Abra woke up with the worst migraine she had ever experienced. Her vision was blurry, and she was disoriented. When she was finally able to see, she thought she would pass out again. Her hands were bound to some sort of railing. She wiggled her body towards it. She pushed her body up against the railing and looked through the frigid, black, metal bars. Once her eyes focused and she realized what was on the other side of those bars, she instantly started hyperventilating and gasping for air. She thrashed around, screaming, trying to escape from the ropes. She had to be 15 stories high. The last thing she remembered before she lost consciousness again was the sound of footsteps and a flash of light.

FIVE MONTHS EARLIER

Abra Ryan sat on her sofa and stared at her husband, Blaine, playing with their two young daughters, Ellie and Norah. She looked around and sighed. She was starting to feel claustrophobic in their tiny apartment.

"Blaine, I've been thinking," she said. Blaine looked at her and raised his eyebrow. "About what?" he asked.

"Well, I've been graduated for a couple of years now, and I haven't done anything with my degree." Abra had received her Masters in Early Childhood Education from the University of Akron three years ago. Right when she was starting to search for a job, she found out she was pregnant with their first child, Ellie. She became so comfortable with being a stay-at-home mom that once Ellie became a little older, she and Blaine decided to have another baby. They were soon blessed with Norah. Now that Norah was a little older, Abra thought now would be the perfect time to start her career.

"That's because you wanted to stay here to be with the girls. You know you can get a job whenever you're ready. I just thought you liked staying home with the girls."

"I do. I just think it's time for a change. I think now's a good time for me to start looking for work."

"Were you thinking about applying around here, or did you want to move?"

"I was thinking this might be a good time for us to move. I mean, other than your job, we have nothing really keeping us here. What would you think about moving down to the Outer Banks? You know, closer to your family?"

Abra knew Blaine would be up for that idea. She remembered how hard it was for him when he had to move up north and leave his family and the beach behind.

"Are you serious? That would be fantastic! Are you sure?" Blaine was practically jumping up and down like a little kid.

"I would have to find a job before we can make anything official, but I think now's the perfect time. Do you think you could talk to Sam to see if there would be an opening for you at the fire department down there?"

"Absolutely! I'll call him later today," Blaine said. Blaine worked with Sam Johnson on the fire department in Nags Head before Blaine met Abra and he moved in with her in Akron. Sam and Blaine had been best friends for years. They still kept in touch a couple of times a week.

Abra and Blaine met when Abra was on vacation with her family at the Outer Banks. They rented a cottage in Kitty Hawk. Sadie convinced Abra to go hang gliding. After hours of peer pressure, Abra got strapped up and darted off the dune. Just as she started running, she tripped. She nose-dived into the sand and was dragged down the beach.

Blaine was an EMT at the time, and just so happened to be on the beach with his friends and saw Abra being dragged. He ran over to help her. He asked if she was okay, and then called for the ambulance. Sadie felt terrible for forcing Abra to go in the first place. She tried to comfort Abra while they waited for the ambulance to arrive.

Sadie rode in the back of the ambulance with Abra and called their parents on the way to the hospital. Later that evening, Abra's parents, Leah and Aaron, were in the hospital room with her when a man with tattoos up and down his arms that looked like a shirt sleeve walked in with a stuffed bear. Abra's parents had no idea who the guy was and tried to get him out of the room and away from their daughter as soon as possible. Abra recognized him right away and told her parents he was the guy who helped her. Abra was delighted when she saw the cute bear. It was the sweetest thing any man had ever done for her. Abra thought about that day frequently. She would think about how, if Sadie had not pressured her into hang gliding, and she herself hadn't been so accident- prone, she might never have met Blaine. She owed Sadie a big thanks for that.

Blaine and Abra had to move quickly to fit in a first date, being that Abra's family was only going to be at the beach for a week. Abra had to stay at the cottage and rest her broken ankle the majority of the time. She told her family she didn't want to ruin their vacations, and they should go out and enjoy their time at the beach.

The last afternoon, the family decided to go visit a couple of the lighthouses. Abra hobbled out onto the back deck with a Nicholas Sparks book. She laid out on a lawn chair and soaked up the sun as she read about a young couple falling in love.

She had been reading for about an hour when she heard hollering coming from down below the deck on the beach. Abra looked down over the edge, and there stood Blaine, waving like a maniac. Abra smiled and waved back. Blaine ran over and scaled the steps and hopped up on the deck.

"What are you doing here?" Abra asked, smiling.

"I was just in the area. I didn't know you were staying here," he said, looking at the house. "It looks like a really nice cottage. How's the ankle doing?" Blaine asked.

"It's starting to feel better, thanks."

"I probably shouldn't stick around. I know your folks weren't too happy to see me the other day at the hospital."

Abra waved the thought away with her hand. "Don't worry about them. They're out sightseeing all day." She looked down at her broken ankle. "I'm the weakest link," she continued. Blaine gave her a sympathetic look.

After they talked for a while, Blaine asked Abra out on a date.

"I would love to, but I'm supposed to stay off my feet, and my family and I will be heading back home early tomorrow morning."

Blaine thought about it for a minute. "How late do you think your family will be out today?"

"They just left not too long ago, so I think they'll be gone for a while."

Blaine looked down at his watch. "Okay, give me a half an hour," he said.

"For what?"

"I have to get ready for our date." He smiled.

"What do you mean? I can't leave. Plus, have you seen what I'm wearing?" Abra said, looking down at her cutoff shorts and old, faded tank top.

"You look beautiful," Blaine said, hopping off of the deck.

Twenty minutes later, he returned with a bag full of KFC. Abra thought it was the worst idea for a first date ever, but Blaine looked so adorable she couldn't turn him down. He handed her the bag of food with one hand and brought his hand out from behind him, revealing a beautiful bouquet of flowers. Abra graciously took the flowers and tried to stand up to put them in water.

"Don't even think about it. Sit back down." He ran inside, grabbed a cup, put water in it, and brought it back out. He took the flowers from Abra, put them in the water and set them on the table next to her. "I'm sorry I can't take you out on a proper date, but we both have to eat, right?"

Abra looked at her watch. "But it's three o'clock in the afternoon," she said, laughing.

"I know, but I didn't know how much time we would have, and I wanted to make the most of it." Blaine started unpacking fried chicken, mashed potatoes and biscuits.

"You do realize there are only two of us, right?" Abra asked.

Blaine looked at all of the food. "What? This is just a snack," he joked.

Abra couldn't help but ask about all of Blaine's tattoos. He pointed at a tattoo of a helmet with an F7 in the middle of it on his right arm.

"I got this one when I first joined the department and they gave me my badge number." He had flames starting under the helmet going all the way down to his hand. He switched to his left arm. "This is the maltese cross," he explained. Abra recognized the firefighter symbol. "I just got this one a couple of months ago. After a bad call a group of us on the department all decided to get this tattoo." Abra was touched by Blaine's commitment to the department.

They had been talking for hours before they heard the car pull in the driveway. Blaine quickly kissed Abra on the cheek and jumped off of the deck and disappeared. Abra leaned back in her chair, not able to contain her smile.

It was now years later, and Abra couldn't be happier. She had a wonderful husband and two beautiful, perfect daughters. She was thrilled to begin the exciting process of job hunting. She created a profile on a site that would hopefully result in getting her job interviews near the Outer Banks. She also submitted resumes to some of the schools in the Nags Head area.

It wasn't too long after she posted her resume that Abra received a phone call from Nags Head Elementary telling her they were interested in meeting her and wanted to know when she could schedule an interview. They wanted her to come in sometime the following day. Abra had to explain that she lived out of town. The lady scheduling the interview was very understanding and agreed to having her come down by the end of the week.

Once Abra scheduled her interview, Blaine and she decided to go down and stay with Blaine's parents for a couple of days, so Abra could go to her interview. Blaine was able to get a couple of days off work, so everything seemed to fall right into place. While they were down there, they also decided to look around the area for houses for sale.

Everything was happening so quickly that Abra's head was starting to spin. Abra and Blaine tried to get packed as fast as they could, so they could get down to Nags Head as quickly as possible. Abra viciously tore through her closet, trying to find something that would hide her post-baby bump. After a year and what seemed to be endless hours of exercise DVDs, she was still not in the same shape she was before she became pregnant with Norah. She recalled that it hadn't taken this long to lose the weight after Ellie was born two years ago. That weight seemed to melt off like butter. She made a mental note to find a new gym once they moved.

Abra looked at the three mounds of clothes in disgust. The first pile contained maternity clothes; the second, clothes she could fit in; and third, clothes she wished she could fit in. Unfortunately, her wish pile seemed to contain almost half of her wardrobe.

Ellie was helping Abra pick out her outfit by jumping in the clothes piles as if they were a mound of leaves. She then hopped off the bed and grabbed Abra's bright pink lipstick sitting on the nightstand and started drawing all over her face.

"Oh Ellie, what am I going to do with you?" Abra smiled and shook her head at her daughter. Ellie looked up at her with a huge grin on her face that resembled a clown. Abra picked her up and took her into the bathroom. She lifted her up onto the counter so she could see herself in the mirror. Ellie was captivated by her reflection. She reached toward it, turned her head to Abra, and said "Look!," which came out "ook!" Abra grabbed a wet towel. "Come here little Bozo," Abra said, wiping off Ellie's face. She then put Ellie back on the ground and returned to her fashion emergency.

She held up the remaining two dresses and asked, "Which one should Mommy wear for her big interview?" Ellie reached out for the loose dress with sleeves. "That's exactly what I was thinking. Black may be slimming, but it's not an eraser." Abra sighed heavily and hung the all-too-fitting dress in her closet. She hung the dress she was going to wear in a garment bag and grabbed her jewelry box. She walked over to the bed and pushed a pile of clothes out of the way in order to sit next to Ellie, who had climbed back into the pile. Ellie snatched a necklace from the box and struggled to get it over her head. Abra helped her put the necklace around her neck and told her how pretty she looked.

She went back to the box and poked around to see which jewelry she should pack to wear to the interview. She tried it on, carefully keeping her jet black curls from catching in the clasp. She walked into the bathroom connected to their master bedroom and strategically applied her lipstick, blush, and mascara. Once she was finally satisfied, she took one last look in the mirror, striking a pose. She grabbed Ellie and tossed her up above her head. Ellie started laughing hysterically.

Abra went into the living room with Ellie--or, as Blaine liked to call her, 'Abra's little shadow.' Over the past couple of months, the only person Ellie wanted was Abra. Blaine took it personally at first. Abra told him over and over that it was just a phase, but it still bothered him. Luckily, she was starting to grow out of that phase and was starting to ask for Blaine more now.

Once everyone was packed for their trip, they headed out the door. Even though they were only going to be gone for a couple of days, their Tahoe looked like they were going away for a year.

Blaine carried their bags down while Abra carried Norah and held Ellie's hand. As Abra struggled getting the two girls down the stairs, she realized more and more that she would not miss the apartment when they moved. Their tiny apartment was on the top floor of their complex, so it was always a hassle dragging groceries up and down the steps and all the way to the far side of the parking lot to get to their Tahoe.

Chapter 2

Blaine had his parents pick them up at the airport. Even though it was a long drive from the nearest airport, it was better than twelve hours with the two girls in the car. Blaine's mom almost knocked him over as she ran towards him and tackled him.

"I'm so glad that you, Abra, and the girls are moving back! I knew you couldn't stay away from the beach," she said excitedly.

"It's not for sure yet, Ma. Abra just has an interview. We'll see how it goes; but, I have all the confidence in the world in my wife," he said, kissing Abra on the head.

"I'm sure she'll get it," Blaine's mom said, hugging Abra.

"So good to see you, Pat," Abra said, hugging her mother-in-law.

"Hey Dad," Blaine said, shaking his dad's hand then pulling him in for a hug.

"Your mother has been talking about you moving here nonstop since you called the other night," he said, chuckling.

"That is so sweet. I really hope we can move down here. I know it would mean a lot to Blaine to be back home and closer to family."

"Welcome home. Both of you,"

"Thanks, Jack. It's great to be here," Abra said, hugging her father-in-law.

Blaine's parents lived in a beautiful home right on the beach. When Abra walked in and looked at the view outside, she was in complete awe at the beauty. She brought Norah and Ellie over to the window to look out. "Look at the beautiful ocean," Abra said, pointing out the window. "Can you say ocean?" Abra asked Ellie. "o-sin" Ellie repeated. "Good job, Ellie!" She turned to Blaine. "Why would you *ever* move away from here?" Blaine gave her a sarcastic smirk. Abra knew very well it was not Blaine's choice to move. If he had his way, he would have stayed there at the beach.

Blaine then shot Abra a smile. "I got a much better offer," he responded.

"Good answer," Jack chimed in, walking up behind him.

Abra looked out the window and was mesmerized by the water. She could see a couple of boats off in the distance. She could definitely get used to this view.

"I was just gonna start some dinner, Abra. Would you like to help me?" Pat asked. Abra handed Ellie to Blaine and followed Pat into the kitchen.

"What are we making?" Abra asked, once they were in the kitchen.

"Fried chicken and macaroni & cheese. Blaine would always ask me to make this for him when he was growing up. When he called and told me you would be staying with us, I ran right out and bought everything I needed. I knew I had to make it for him his first night back."

"That's very thoughtful," Abra responded. In the back of her mind, she couldn't help but think that maybe Blaine's mom didn't realize he wasn't five years old anymore. The way she was talking made it sound like Blaine would be moving back in with his parents.

While Abra was at her interview the following day, Blaine stayed home and spent time with his family.

They spent the majority of the day on the beach with Ellie and Norah.

Pat watched the girls while Blaine and Jack went fishing. It reminded Blaine of when he was little. Blaine and his dad would go fishing almost every weekend. He had never told Abra this, but when she was pregnant with both girls, he had secretly wished they would be boys. He loved his daughters very much, and wouldn't trade them for the world, but he thought it would be nice to have a son he could share things with. Now he just hoped either Ellie or Norah would like to fish or play sports so they would have something they could bond over like Blaine and his father.

Blaine absolutely loved the ocean and anything to do with it. He had taken to boats the way most guys took to cars. To mention a Ferrari or a Lamborghini did nothing for him, but take him out on the water and he could name any watercraft around. Although boats were his particular interest, he loved everything about the ocean: the water, the sand, the boogie boarding...if it was at the beach, he loved it. Blaine's father was the same way. Blaine's favorite memories growing up were sitting outside, watching all the life, and fishing with his dad.

When Abra came home that evening, Blaine asked her how the interview went.

"It went fine. You know. I won't hear anything for a while," she said.

Blaine could tell something was wrong, but he didn't want to press her in front of everyone. Blaine knew Abra felt a certain amount of pressure in front of his parents.

Later that night, when they were alone in his old bedroom, Blaine asked her about the interview again.

"I told you, it went just fine," she said, but their was an edge in her voice. "Do you think you got the job?" he asked.

"I don't know Blaine. I'm sure there are a lot of other great candidates," she snapped back.

"Abra, what happened? Something's wrong."

"I don't want to talk about it right now, okay?" She said coldly. Blaine decided he was better off to just drop it.

The next morning, Pat made a large breakfast for everyone before Blaine and Abra had to pack up all of their things to head to the airport and catch their plane.

Abra was starting to get nervous. It had been a couple of weeks since her job interview, and she still hadn't heard back from the school.

"I thought you said the interview went great," Blaine responded one night after Abra mentioned her concerns about not hearing back from the school. Blaine had been waiting for Abra to bring it up since the day of the interview. He knew something went wrong, but she refused to talk about it, and he knew not to push it. Abra had been too embarrassed to talk about the interview up to this point.

She took a deep breath, "Well..." she trailed off.

"What happened?" He asked.

That was when Abra finally broke down.

"I made a fool of myself. I flubbed up answers, sweated profusely. It was a complete disaster!" Abra finally allowed herself to unravel in front of Blaine. All of the emotions that had been building up inside of her since the interview erupted like lava in a volcano.

"Oh, Sweetie, why didn't you say anything?"

"I was too embarrassed," she cried.

He took her in his arms.

"Don't worry. They would be fools not to hire you, but if they don't, it's okay. You can keep applying to jobs and continue staying with the girls until you find the right school for you."

"But that's the only school with an opening near your family. I really wanted to get it so you could be by your family again."

Blaine nodded. "It would be nice to be back home, but we've lived away from them for years now. I've kinda gotten used to being away from them. You should never feel embarrassed to talk to me. I'm your husband. That's what I'm here for," he took her hand in his and kissed it.

"Thanks. I don't know what I would do without you." Abra said

"Then it's a good thing you'll never have to find out," he joked, and squeezed her tightly.

They sat on the couch and he held her for a while. Just like that, Abra's problems dissolved. Blaine had an incredible ability to make things right again. No matter how awful anything was in Abra's life, Blaine was able to fix it with just the touch of his hand. She immediately felt silly for not telling him about the interview in the first place.

The next morning, Abra was playing with Ellie and Norah in their tiny living room/dining room when her cell phone rang. Just as the lady on the other end of the line said she was from Nags Head Elementary, Ellie hit the button on the toy she was playing with, causing it to play a really loud, obnoxious tune. Abra quickly grabbed it, turned it off and handed Ellie her favorite doll, Heidi. Ellie grabbed her with both hands and squeezed her tightly.

"Mrs. Ryan, this is Kate from Nags Head Elementary. We wanted to let you know that after careful consideration, we would like to offer you the job if you are still interested." Abra silently jumped up and down. Ellie, getting a kick out of the scene, started jumping up and down too, trying to mimic her mom.

"Yes, of course! Thank you so much!"

"Terrific! We will need you to come in Monday so we can show you around and get all the paperwork filled out. Congratulations, and welcome aboard." Abra thanked her again and hung up the phone.

"Blaine, Blaine!" She hollered out.

Blaine rushed in. "What's the matter?" He asked in a panicked tone.

"I got the job!" She squealed.

Blaine grabbed her around the waist and lifted her up. She wrapped her legs around his waist and squeezed him tightly. "Congratulations! I'm so happy for you!" He kissed her. "I knew you could do it! I told you there was nothing to worry about."

"There's one problem though. They need me to come in on Monday."

"Okay, we'll go down and stay with my parents again. I'm sure they won't mind."

"Okay, but what about the girls? If I'm starting back at the department, and you're working too, who's going to watch Norah and Ellie?" Abra asked, playfully tossing Norah in the air.

"We could check out local day cares?" Blaine suggested.

Abra sat down with Norah in her lap. She grabbed her laptop that was sitting next to her and Googled day cares in the Nags Head area while Blaine entertained the girls. She found a lot of different results, but only a couple of them were actually close enough to consider. She clicked on the first link and was taken to a page with shapes dancing back and forth. She clicked the button that read TEACHERS. Right away a picture of a lady in her early thirties popped up. She had a gigantic smile and saucer-like eyes. *Who would trust someone like that with their children?* She thought to herself. She quickly went back to the search result page and went to the next link. This one had a picture of a lady in her twenties. She had a pretty smile and her eyes were normal sized. Abra pulled up their mission statement and read what they were about and everything they offered.

"This sounds like a really nice place." She announced out loud.

"Find something?" Blaine asked, looking over Abra's shoulder.

"Maybe," Abra said slowly, clicking on the cost button. She immediately felt her eyes get as big as the lady's from the first daycare. "If we went with this place, it would probably cost my whole paycheck in order to afford it," Abra said, feeling dejected.

"Keep looking. There's got to be a place that's less expensive." There were still more links to check out so Abra went through a mental checklist as she scrolled through the next site. Normal photo: check, offers good educational tools for kids: check, affordable: check. Blaine and Abra both agreed, and

Abra picked up her cell phone off the desk and punched in the number.

"Thank you for calling Kids First Day Care."

"Hi, my name is Abra Ryan. My husband and I are looking for day care for our two daughters."

"Ooh, I'm sorry ma'am. We are currently full. We have a waiting list that goes out about eight months." The lady said with a southern accent. Abra thanked her and hung up.

"What are we going to do now?" Blaine asked as Abra hung up her phone, sensing from Abra's tone that that daycare wasn't going to work for them.

"I guess we'll have to find someone like a nanny or a sitter to watch them at the house."

Blaine was now on all fours with Ellie on his back. Ellie was swinging her arm above her head, pretending she was lassoing a horse. Norah was sleeping in Abra's lap.

"I'm gonna put her down for her nap," Abra told Blaine. Blaine neighed loudly in response. Ellie threw her head back and laughed hysterically. Abra quietly made her way through the hall to the nursery and laid Norah down in her crib. Once Abra laid her down, Norah stirred and fussed for a minute, then rolled to her side and fell back asleep. Abra looked down in awe and smiled at how sweet and peaceful Norah looked. Abra went back to the living room and curled up on the couch with her laptop. She went to a website that was designed to help working parents find babysitters and nanny's. She created a profile and hoped for the best.

Blaine and Abra searched every realtor's website to see what houses were for sale. Blaine called Sam up and he said they would absolutely love to have him back on the department.

Blaine talked to his parents and they said him, Abra, Ellie, and Norah could stay with them until they were able to find a place of their own, so they packed up once again and headed down south.

Chapter 3

In a neighboring city, a fiery redhead stepped outside in her yoga pants and a hoodie to get her morning newspaper. She had had the same routine for the past five years: wake up at six, do an hour of yoga, followed by catching up on current events while she enjoyed her morning coffee. She poured herself a hot cup of Italian Roast, sat at the table, and leafed through the pages. As she read through all of the tragedies and excitement from the day before, something caught her attention. All of a sudden a wave of memories washed over her. *He's back!* She thought. She was completely overwhelmed with emotions. After all of this time, she was finally going to get a second chance. She would not screw this up again.

She quickly rushed into her bedroom and opened the closet. She reached up on the top shelf and pulled down what looked like a photo album. She carried it back out to the kitchen table, set it down, walked over to the desk, and rummaged through the drawer until she found tape, scissors, a Sharpie marker and a pen. She went back out to the kitchen, sat down at the table, and opened the scrapbook to the next unused page. The last things in the scrapbook were a couple of newspaper clippings from a couple of years ago. One was a wedding announcement. Next to it were two birth announcements that had been printed off of the internet. It had become a daily habit to Google his name just to see if anything would show up. That was how she found out everything she knew about him. The fact that he was working as a dispatcher for a fire department in Ohio, had gotten married, and had two children. She looked down at the book. The edge of the wedding announcement was starting to curl up and peel up at the edges, revealing Abra's face. She added more two-sided tape and pushed down hard on top of the face, covering it with a picture of her own.

She picked up the newspaper and scissors and carefully cut out the ad in the classifieds, adding it to the next blank page in the book. *Abra,* she thought, *what a dumb name!* She picked up the Sharpie and blacked out the name, then she grabbed the pen and wrote her own name above it.

When she finished, she sat back in her chair and took another sip of coffee. She reached in the pocket of her hoodie and pulled out her cell phone. She scanned the page one more time for the contact number. She plugged in the number from the ad and saved it as one of her favorites in her contact list. She shoved her phone back in her pocket and closed the book. She sat there for a while, finishing her coffee, staring out the window and planning her next move.

It was times like these that made her crave a bagel with cream cheese or a delicious danish. *No!* She scolded herself. She was through giving into carbs and sugars. She had done too well for too long to let it slip away so quickly. Now when she strolled down the street people mistook her for a model. She constantly caught guys giving her a double take, which was often followed by their wives or girlfriends slapping them and yelling at them. That was not the case a couple of years ago. Sure, she turned heads back in high school as well, but for a completely different reason. She put her scrapbook away, grabbed her bath towel hanging off the back of the door and jumped in the shower before heading out to get some work done.

She had worked as a freelance photographer for the past five years and absolutely loved it. She loved the fact that she didn't have to answer to a boss, or have a typical nine-to-five job. That was too monotonous and was definitely not for her. She also lived in the perfect place to be a photographer. She had some clients who were couples getting married on the beach. Watching all of these couples getting married made her a little bitter, but other than that she loved her job. Plus, that was how she would get ideas for her wedding. She had it all planned out, down to the groom. He just didn't know it yet.

Abra was still caught off guard by the ocean breeze when she opened the back door of Blaine's parents' house. She wasn't sure whether it was the saltiness, the moist, warm air, or the ocean smell, but it still caught her off guard every single time.

Ellie ran out the door ahead of Abra towards Blaine, who was sitting on the deck holding Norah. Ellie patted Norah on the head and then quickly got distracted by the beach.

"How's the water looking today?" Abra asked, sitting down on the wooden chair beside Blaine.

He smiled. "It's really been active this morning. I saw a school of porpoises way out there. There had to be twenty of them. They were jumping all over the place!" He handed her his binoculars so she could see them.

"Oh, wow," she said softly in amazement as she watched the porpoises rise just above the surface and gracefully dive back down.

Blaine carried on in great detail to Abra about all of the different boats and jet skis that were cruising the ocean that morning.

Abra rolled her eyes. "I swear, if you had it your way, we would just moved into a houseboat," she giggled. Blaine opened his eyes really wide.

"Was that an option?" he asked excitedly.

"No!" she said quickly, laughing.

"Hey, you knew this about me when you married me!" he joked. Blaine had a picture of a beautiful yacht that was his dream boat that he kept set aside. It was a Cruiser, which resembled a house on water. It had everything they could ever need or want. It even had speakers scattered throughout for surround sound. Blaine could just picture his family relaxing on the yacht. He was going to own that yacht someday. He just had to convince Abra. Plus win the lottery.

Blaine and Abra sat on the deck for a little while, watching as a sailboat elegantly floated along until a gang of wave runners crashed through like an aquatic biker gang, rocking the sailboat, almost tipping it over.

The house hunting process had been horrible. It was filled with arguments like, "Just pick one!" and "We have to find something. We can't live with your parents forever!" But when they stepped into what would become their house, it was magical. As they walked through the halls and toured the rooms, they immediately started pointing out where they wanted to put furniture and how they were going to decorate. They could instantly see themselves raising their family there. "Welcome home," Abra had whispered to Blaine.

The house was beautiful. Two story, not too far from the beach. It had a balcony and a deck on the ground floor with a hot tub. The bedrooms were all on the first floor and the living room, dining room, and kitchen were all on the second floor.

Finally, it was moving day. Abra took it all in as they drove through their new neighborhood, looking for grocery stores, Wal-Marts, or Targets that she would be able to shop at. A U-haul truck drove down their long gravel driveway. Trailing right behind it was the Ryan's Tahoe. Blaine and Abra jumped out and went to take their daughters out of their car seats. Ellie started unbuckling herself while Norah waited not-so-patiently for her dad's help.

As they walked up to their house, Blaine wrapped his free arm around Abra. She looked over and smiled.

"Are you ready?" Blaine asked, reaching for his keychain.

Abra took a deep breath, "I've been looking forward to this moment for years."

Blaine took Ellie from Abra. "Wait here," he ordered. He set Ellie and Norah in the house, then ran back out and picked Abra up and carried her over the threshold. "I've been waiting years to be able to do that," he said, excitedly. Still carrying her, he ran over and tossed her on the couch the movers had just set down. Abra shrieked playfully and then laughed and popped up off the couch. He took her hand and twirled her, pulled her in, dipped her and gave her a kiss.

"I'm so glad we finally got out of that teensy apartment! The girls finally have room to run around and play." Abra commented.

"This is going to be a wonderful new start," Blaine replied.

"Uh, guys, these boxes aren't getting any lighter," a large man wearing a back brace pointed out.

"Sorry, George," Blaine said, stepping out of the way so the mover could go inside. Blaine was starting to follow him when Abra hollered after him.

"Wait! There's something I want to do," Abra said. She ran back outside to the end of the driveway. She yanked the realtor sign with the giant letters SOLD covering the sign out of the ground. She turned towards Blaine and raised it over her head in victory. Blaine cheered. Abra ran back to the house. "Sorry, I've always wanted to do that."

Abra began unpacking dishes and pots and pans, trying to decide how she wanted to organize her kitchen while also chasing the girls around. Blaine was working in the living room, trying to setup their entertainment center. The burly mover came tromping up the steps.

"Ma'am?" He asked, looking down at the heavy box in his arms.

Abra pointed, "Second door on the right. Thanks, George."

The man took off down the stairs. He returned a few minutes later wiping his brow with a hankie from his pocket. "Johnny is bringing in one more box, and then I think that's the end of it."

Blaine jumped up and jogged into the kitchen. He reached in his pocket to take out his wallet and handed him money. "Thanks again," Blaine said. The mover nodded, took the money and tromped back down the stairs.

"Can you believe it?" Abra twirled around the kitchen. "Our own home!"

"I know! It's incredible!" He walked up behind her, placing his hands on her waist. She looked up at him and kissed him lightly on the lips.

"I can't wait to start our new life together," she whispered. "I know it's going to be wonderful."

That night, Blaine, Abra, Ellie and Norah spent the evening outside on the beach. Ellie was standing barefoot in the sand. She revealed a big, toothy smile and giggled. She picked her foot up slowly and then stomped it down hard. Her tiny mouth formed an "O" in amazement, and she pointed at her footprint. Blaine was holding Norah. He knelt down and put her feet in the sand. Norah, on the other hand was completely repulsed by the wet, mushy sand sticking to the bottoms of her feet. The instant it touched her tiny feet, her lip curled out, her eyes welled up with tears, and she screamed bloody murder. Blaine immediately picked her up and brushed the sand off. Ellie hobbled over to the blanket they laid out and grabbed the pacifier and held it up to Norah.

"What a great big sister you are, Ellie," Blaine praised. Ellie started bouncing up and down clapping excitedly.

Abra laid on the blanket and marveled in awe at her family. Everything was finally coming together for them. She already had the perfect family and now the house that she had always dreamed of. She couldn't think of a more peaceful place to raise her family.

That night they put the girls to bed early. Afterwards, Blaine looked at Abra. "You know, we almost forgot the most important thing about moving into a new house."

"Oh yeah, what's that?"

"Christening it," he said, raising his eyebrows at her.

"How could we have ever forgotten that? That would have been such a shame."

"True, and I read somewhere if you don't, you're doomed with like ten years of flooding."

"Well, we can't let that happen, now can we?"

Blaine reached up to Abra's hair and took a strand of her onyx curls and wrapped it around his finger. Abra had the most beautiful hair Blaine had ever seen. It was one of the first things he had noticed about her, besides her shattered ankle. He let the hair fall loose from his finger and watched as it sprang back into place. He led her into their bedroom and playfully tossed her on the bed.

Abra and Blaine spent the whole next day finding a new home for their belongings until it was time to put the girls to bed. Abra bathed Ellie and Norah and put them in their pajamas. She told Ellie to go over to their bookshelf and pick out a book to read that night. Abra loved cuddling with them and holding them close as she read to them, and Ellie loved when Abra let her turn the pages. Whenever Abra finished reading a page, Ellie would excitedly turn the page and look up at Abra and smile a big, beautiful smile. This was the highlight of Abra's day.

Norah and Ellie shared a bedroom. Even though there was another spare bedroom in the house, Abra felt the girls would become closer friends if they shared a room growing up, so they turned the extra room into an office for Abra. Abra and her sister had shared a room when they were little, and Abra felt that had brought them closer together. She had so many wonderful memories growing up with her sister, Sadie: whispering stories to each other after their parents had thought they were both fast asleep, doing each other's hair and nails, talking about boys. Abra and her sister had always been best friends. That was until...Abra shook her head, trying to erase the memories like an Etch A Sketch. However, no matter how hard she tried, there were always tiny particles left behind that never fully disappeared.

Blaine didn't realize how much he missed the fire department until he stepped back into his old station. He was flooded with memories from all of the hours he spent there. All of the laughs and sometimes the tears shared among his firefighter family. He knew it wasn't something anyone could understand unless they had experienced it themselves. He thought about the night he was called for what turned out to be an arson. Two young children and their mother all burned alive. Everyone understood the tragedy of it all, but no one could possibly comprehend the feeling of being the first one on the scene. Trying to save someone and the horror of realizing you were failing. The only ones who could fully understand are your firefighter family.

Blaine saw the chief was in his office, so he walked over and knocked on the side of the door. "Ryan," the chief called out and jumped out of his swivel chair to go shake Blaine's hand.

"Good to see you, Chief," Blaine responded.

"When Sam told me you were moving back to town, I couldn't believe it. You were one of the best firefighters I've seen. We're all thrilled to have you back."

"Thank you, sir. It's great to be back."

"Let's get you your gear. Lucky for you, I think yours is still available. Assuming you haven't packed on too much weight, they should still work." Blaine went to the garage and grabbed his old fire gear off of the hook. The chief came out and handed Blaine his radio. "You'll have to come to the next fire practice. They're still on Monday nights at seven o'clock."

"I'll be there. I've been looking forward to getting back into it."

Monday night, Blaine went to fire practice. Sam was there already waiting for him. "Hey, man," he called out reaching his hand out for a fist bump.

That night they were doing a live burn. They would light fires in different rooms of an old abandoned house and they would take turns going in to put it out. Blaine put on his air mask. He forgot how awkward and uncomfortable they were. They only produce air when you need it, so for a brief moment you feel like you're suffocating. Blaine crawled through the house with Sam trailing behind him. They crawled around in pure darkness, feeling around to figure out their bearings. There were some ropes lying around on the ground. One of them got caught on Blaine's foot and tightened. He was stuck. He began to panic, causing him to use more oxygen then he should have. At the last minute, Sam reached for his knife and cut the rope, releasing Blaine's foot. They quickly made their way out of the house.

"What took you guys so long?" The chief asked, looking at his stopwatch.

"I got my foot stuck in some rope. Sam had to cut my foot out," Blaine explained.

"It's been a while. I've been dispatching so long I guess I'm a little rusty."

The chief nodded. "Just try to do better next time."

Blaine was thrilled to be back on the department where he had started out. Being handed his radio and fire gear was like being handed an award. His schedule would be four twelve hour days, followed by three midnight shifts in a row. He would have three days off before it would start all over again. Sam was on the same shift, which was something they were both happy about.

When Blaine showed up for his first shift, Sam was already there, standing by his truck. He called Blaine over. As Blaine walked towards him, he asked, "What's going on?" Sam pulled a box off of his passenger side seat and handed it to Blaine. Blaine looked at it suspiciously. "What's this?" he asked.

"Just open it," Sam replied. It was a knife.

"If you're gonna be back on the department, you're gonna need one of these. I'm not always gonna be there to get you out of trouble."

Blaine chuckled, "Thanks man." They walked into the station together. If he was going to be spending this much time away from his family, it made Blaine feel a little better knowing he would be spending it with a good friend.

The next morning, Abra heard a cell phone ring from the other room. As she walked towards the living room, she heard Blaine talking, and it became obvious it was Pat. "We would love for you to come see the house. How about if you, Dad, Charlie, Ana, and the boys come over tomorrow night for dinner?"

Abra could tell from his response that his mother had agreed. Abra gritted her teeth. *This place is not ready for house guests.* Abra continued to listen to the conversation.

"I'll text Charlie and see if they're free. Yeah, I know things aren't great between them right now. No, I don't know what's going on with them, Mom," he lied. "Okay, Mom, I'll see you tomorrow. Love you. Bye."

Abra stood in the doorway. "You invited your whole family over tomorrow night for dinner without even so much as consulting me? How could you? We are nowhere near ready for people to come over."

"It'll be fine. It's my family, they won't care. We'll get it all finished before they come over. There's not that much left to do," he replied in his annoyingly-calm voice.

"Are you kidding? I wanted to paint the kitchen and dining room, and we still have a million boxes full of things we need to find places for." Abra knew Blaine's family would understand they had just moved in, but she wanted the house to look perfect before they had anyone over. Boxes thrown about were natural in a new home, but this did not stop Abra from having a panic attack about everything they had left to do. She wanted their first guests, her in-laws, to see their new home for the first time when everything was put away and in order.

He placed his hands on hers. "Don't worry about painting. Let's just get everything out of boxes and put away." Abra was about to protest, but he put his finger to her lips. "We have plenty of time to paint. The walls look fine the way they are. We'll have everyone over again after we paint."

"Fine," Abra said, through clenched teeth.

The next night, Blaine's family trailed in. His mom walked in first, ecstatic. "I'm so happy Abra got the job and you've officially moved here." She grabbed his face and pulled it down to hers, kissing him on both cheeks.

"Me too, Ma. It's great to be close to you all again. Thanks for letting us stay with you."

"Of course. Anything for family."

"Hi Pat!" Abra greeted, hugging her mother-in-law.

"So good to see you, Sweetheart! Now where are my favorite granddaughters? I've missed them so much since you left."

"They're your only granddaughters," Blaine reminded her.

"They're still my favorites!" She yelled back. When they reached the top of the stairs, Pat took a look around at the kitchen. "Yuck! I hope you plan on painting." Abra nearly jumped over the counter at her. Blaine grabbed her just in time. Abra shot Blaine a death glare.

"It's okay," he whispered, chuckling under his breath. "Of course we're going to paint, Ma. We just haven't had a chance yet."

By this point, Pat was already out of the kitchen and looking in the other rooms. Just as Blaine followed her, they heard the doorbell.

"That must be Charlie. I'll grab it," Blaine said.

"Hey, Bro! I didn't think we'd ever get to see your place," Charlie jabbed.

"Chill out, we've only been here for one week. We had to get settled first." He turned to his sister-in-law. "Hi, Ana," he greeted.

"Hey, Blaine. Good to see you. Max! Don't run in the house!" She yelled at her eight- year-old son. Blaine jumped at the shrillness in her voice. "Jake, get back here! Where's Abra?" Ana asked calmly.

Her rapid conversation jumps were laughable to Blaine. He pointed up the steps, "Dining room with the rest of the clan."

She grabbed both boys by their arms and dragged them up the steps. "What did I tell you about behaving while you were here?" she asked the boys.

"We don't know how to be-have," Max said. Jake snickered.

"That's it, no X-Box when you get home!"

Both boys lowered their heads.

"Sorry," they said in unison.

Blaine and Charlie stayed downstairs.

"Wanna shoot a quick game of pool?" Charlie asked.

"Shouldn't we join everyone upstairs?" Blaine responded.

"Yeah, but I was kinda hoping to talk to you alone."

"I don't have anything more to say to you than I did the last time we talked."

Charlie cleared his throat. "I know. You probably think I'm a jerk for what I did."

"That's putting it mildly."

"Just a quick game?" Charlie asked again, almost pleading.

"Ok, fine. I'll break." He gathered the balls, racked them, and lined them up on the felt. Charlie handed him a cue stick. "So what did you need to talk to me about?" Blaine asked, sending the cue ball flying across the felt, making a cracking sound as it sent the solid and striped balls scattering in all different directions. One of the solid ones went into the corner pocket. "Solids," Blaine called out, and set up for another shot.

"I broke it off with Gloria. I told her what a mistake that night was and that we could never see each other again."

Blaine nodded. "Good. Does Ana know?"

"Yeah, I told her everything. I told her how Gloria and I slept together that one time. Then I told her I told Gloria we couldn't see each other again."

"Good for you, Charlie."

"I know you may not believe this, but I realize what a huge mistake I've made of my life. I'm doing everything in my power to make things right again."

"I'm glad to hear it. Did Ana forgive you?"

"I hope so. She said she does, but then it seems like any time I make the slightest mistake, even just forgetting to take out the trash, she blows up like a Tomahawk Cruise Missile."

"I'm not going to tell you it's going to be easy. It's going to take a lot of time to mend what you've done. I'm not saying it's not fixable, but it's going to take a lot of work." Charlie took a shot, knocking two stripes in. "But that's not what tonight's about. Tonight we're all together for the first time since Norah was born. Let's celebrate," Blaine said, taking the cue stick from Charlie and laying them both on the table.

He patted Charlie on the shoulder and led him to the dining room. They both grabbed a slice of pepperoni pizza and joined the rest of the family. Blaine looked over at Charlie with his arm around Ana. Blaine knew Charlie loved Ana. That was obvious. So what was it that would cause a man to risk it all over someone he barely knew? Blaine didn't think he would ever be able to understand.

Chapter 4

It was Monday morning. Abra loved the weekends, but they always went by too fast. Especially this particular weekend. Blaine had the next couple of days off, so he was able to watch Norah and Ellie, allowing Abra to go to school to fill out paperwork and get a tour. This was only a temporary fix. They needed to find someone to watch the girls soon.

Blaine was downstairs feeding the girls breakfast when Abra came rushing down the stairs to grab a cup of coffee and leave for orientation. The time had completely gotten away from her. "Thank you so much!" She told Blaine. She hugged and kissed Blaine, Ellie, and Norah, then ran out the door.

Abra was very anxious to get started. She planned out how she wanted to decorate her classroom and created lesson plans in her head. She first went into Kate's office. Kate was hiding behind a stack of papers that she and Abra had to discuss. After about an hour, Abra felt like her brain was going to explode with all the information Kate had been throwing at her. Kate walked her around the school and told her all of her responsibilities and what was required of her as a teacher. By the end of the day, she felt like she had carpal tunnel from filling out all of the paperwork.

Abra was ecstatic to be able to start decorating. She walked into her classroom, taking a look at all of the empty desks as she made her way to the front of the room. She set down her overstuffed canvas bag, and she was pretty sure it weighed the combination of Ellie and Norah together. She started rummaging through the bag to make sure she was completely prepared. She took out all the decorations she wanted to pin up on the walls and the laminated-ruler-shaped name tags. She walked around and taped them to each desk so each student would know where to sit.

Abra walked in the house later that evening and cringed. Walking into Ellie and Norah's bedroom, she wanted to scream. The girls' clothes that Blaine had changed them out of earlier that day were thrown all over the floor. The Diaper Genie was full, but instead of being clean, the dirty diapers were left on the changing table.

Abra made her way through the house as if she was retracing a crime scene. There had obviously been a struggle in the kids' room. Scattered toys led her up the steps to where the imaginary crime would have taken place. It had only been a couple of hours. How could the house be in such a disastrous state in such a short amount of time. She stepped out on the deck and scanned the backyard. There they were. Her beautiful family. Blaine was assisting Ellie in making sand castles in the sandbox Blaine had set up in the back yard. He wished they could buy a house on the beach, but they couldn't afford it. Abra's heart melted at the scene in front of her. *This mess could wait*, she thought to herself and skipped down the stairs and plopped down beside them and started shoveling sand into the empty container lying beside her to contribute to the village they were building.

The next time Blaine started afternoon shifts, Abra used it as an opportunity to go out on the beach and search for seashells and sea glass for some projects she was working on. She had to get on the beach early before other seashell and sea glass collectors got out there and snatched up the good finds. She woke up just as the sun was starting to rise. She grabbed the bucket they used to make sand castles. Abra loved how peaceful it was walking along the beach. It was such a tranquil way to begin a hectic day with her two busy daughters. She found a handful of small pieces of sea glass and quite a few shells. Once her bucket was full, she went back home, washed off the sea glass, and was able to fill an empty baby food jar. She hot glued the lid on and set it on the bookshelf in Ellie and Norah's room.

Abra spent the rest of the week looking for a nanny. By Thursday, she had become very discouraged about the prospects of finding a nanny who would be good enough to look after her daughters. She had countless interviews of girls and women seeking work, but none of them seemed right. She knew it would be difficult finding someone she could trust to watch her daughters, but she hadn't realized it was going to seem so impossible.

"Don't worry, girls, I'm going to find you the best nanny there is!" she told Ellie and Norah as she made her way to the door. "Hi, you must be Francine," Abra greeted the lady.

She was slightly taller than Abra with sandy blonde hair pulled back in a bun so tight that it made her eyes look like they were injected with Botox. She was wearing a brown skirt that went just past her knees and a plain, off-white blouse. "Yes, I am Francine Carlton." She responded plainly.

"So nice to meet you. Why don't we have a seat?" Abra gestured, stepping aside to let her in. Once they were seated, Abra looked over Francine's resume. Abra was filled with a quiet satisfaction that she was no longer in the interview hot seat. "Why don't you tell me a little about yourself?" Abra began. No matter how many times she asked someone that, she still smiled inside.

"I have been a nanny for ten years. Over that time I have worked with many families."   "That's wonderful," Abra said, then paused, waiting for her to continue.

"Do you have any kids yourself?" Abra asked.

"No," she said simply.

"You must really love children if you were willing to make them your career."

"Yes, children bring me a lot of joy," she said dryly. *Clearly*, Abra thought, but refrained from saying. Abra stood up and extended her hand.

"Okay, thanks for coming. I'll get back to you soon," she said and led her to the door. Once Francine left, Abra closed the door and backed up into it, "I'm NEVER going to find a nanny!" Abra said out loud to herself.

After three-and-a-half days of interviews, Abra was exhausted and frustrated. She was just about to give up hope when the doorbell rang. It was the last interview scheduled for the day. Her name was Jan Marsh and she was, without a doubt, the most upbeat and perky woman Abra had ever met. "It's so nice to meet you!" Jan said, excitedly pumping Abra's hand. Abra couldn't help but laugh. Her peppiness was refreshing. Abra stepped aside, let Jan in, and led her up the stairs to the kitchen table.

They sat down and Abra started firing questions at her, which Jan answered perfectly. "I have a degree in early childhood education. I love to cook and clean. I'm kind of a neat freak, so you don't have to worry about ever coming home to a messy house." Abra covered her heart with both of her hands.

"I think I'm in love," she gasped, both of them laughing.

Abra then introduced Jan to Ellie and Norah. Ellie was playing with her baby doll, Heidi. Heidi was Abra's first doll when she was a little girl. When she grew up, she set Heidi aside for her future daughter. She was elated when she found out Ellie was going to be a girl so she could hand Heidi down to her. Ellie absolutely loved Heidi. She never went anywhere without her, so it really took Abra by surprise when Ellie ran over to Jan and held Heidi out to her. Abra took it as a good sign that Ellie approved of Jan. Norah began to stir and fuss in her playpen.

"She's probably hungry." Abra said, reaching in to get her. They walked to the kitchen. Abra grabbed a clean bottle off of the dish rack and filled it up with milk.

"Allow me," Jan offered, reaching out for the baby. Abra handed Norah over to her. Jan situated herself on the sofa and fed Norah while Abra continued asking her questions. There was no doubt about it; Jan was fabulous.

Jan had been there for over an hour. Abra absolutely loved her. She seemed to be the most obvious choice. "Well, Jan, I think I've seen enough. My girls love you, you can cook and clean," she began. Abra was about to offer Jan the job, when Blaine walked in.

"Miss Marsh," Blaine said matter-of-factly. Abra's head whipped back and forth between the two of them like a dog watching a tennis match. Jan looked like a deer in headlights then rushed out of the house so quickly it could have been on fire. Blaine quickly shut the door and secured the dead bolt. Then he ran over to the window and peeked through the shades and watched as she drove off. "What the hell, Abra? Are you just going to let anyone in our house?"

"I don't understand," Abra said, confused.

"The guys at the department all warned me about her. She's psychotic. I've only been on the department a couple of weeks, and I've already been to her house twice." Blaine was still looking out the window. Abra was more than a little shaken up over what just took place and how close she was to offering Jan the job.

Once again they were stuck without a nanny. Abra promised herself she would give it until the end of the week before she would call Kate and tell her she couldn't take the job. That was the last thing she wanted to do right now. After all this time, she finally had the opportunity to start a career. She wasn't going to give that up very easily.

Friday quickly came, and Abra was really beginning to lose all hope that she was ever going to find an acceptable nanny.

She was feeding the girls lunch when the doorbell rang. "That must be the next nanny," she told Ellie. Abra took a quick glance at the list of people she called for an interview that was lying on the table. "Her name is Jenna Richards." She wiped off Norah's face with her bib and grabbed a rag and cleaned Ellie off as best as she could. Somehow the SpaghettiOs Ellie had been eating seemed to make their way all the way up to her forehead.

Abra carried Norah to the front door. She opened the door and was greeted by a tall, slender woman wearing black pants and a dark green blouse. Her red hair was pulled back loosely in a ponytail.

"Hi, I'm Jenna," she said brightly, extending her hand.

"Come on in," Abra welcomed Jenna into the house.

"Hi there, Sweetie," Jenna greeted Ellie, bending over to be closer to her. Ellie made a mischievous smile and turned to run away.

"How old is she?" Jenna asked.

"She's two years and Norah here is one year," Abra said, glancing down in her arms.

"Is she talking yet?" Jenna asked, referring to Norah as Abra lead Jenna upstairs to the kitchen.

"She says a couple of words, but she hasn't said 'Mommy' yet, even though she doesn't seem to have a problem saying 'Dada,'" Abra said, not able to hide the disappointment in her voice. Can I get you something to drink?"

"Sure, just some water would be fine." Abra placed Norah in the Pac 'N Play in the living room and headed to the kitchen with Ellie at her ankles.

Jenna walked over to the Pac 'N Play, kneeled down, and placed her chin in her hands. She stared at Norah with adoration. Norah was holding on tightly to a set of plastic keys and sucking on them. Jenna looked around to make sure Abra was still in the kitchen with Ellie. Jenna reached in and took the keys. Norah immediately started crying. Jenna reached in and picked her up and started playfully bringing the keys closer and further away from her. Norah instantly cheered up and reached out for them. Just then, Abra walked in to see Jenna playing with Norah.

"You're so good with her."

"She was getting a little fussy, so I picked her up. I hope you don't mind. She seemed to be a lot happier when I took her out of there."

"No, that's fine. She seems to really like you. I'll just put your water on the table," Abra said walking towards the dining room.

Jenna was bouncing Norah up and down, making silly faces at her. Norah giggled hysterically. Abra sat down on the sofa, and Jenna, still carrying Norah, sat down beside her.

"So, tell me a little about yourself," Abra forced herself to hide back a grin. She found herself constantly mimicking Kate's questions from her own previous interview.

"Let's see," Jenna began, gazing off into space to search for the words. "I'm 25. I graduated from the University of North Carolina. I'm not married, and I don't have any kids, which means I will be able to be here whenever you need me." She took a drink of water. Abra asked a few more questions before she was convinced she had made her decision.

"I was just hired as a teacher at Nags Head Elementary. My husband works for the fire department, so his shifts vary. We would just need someone during the day. School starts September 5th, so we really need someone to start almost immediately. Will that be a problem?"

"No, not at all. That sounds great!"

"Also, if it's alright, we would like you to spend as much time as possible here this coming weekend while we're here so the girls are able to warm up to you," Abra suggested.

A huge smile came across Jenna's face. "That's a great idea! I know it must be difficult leaving your children with someone new, but I promise you that your girls will be in the best hands possible. I fully believe the smoother the transition we can make for these two angels, the easier it will be on everyone."

"I couldn't agree more," Abra said hopefully. She had a really good feeling about Jenna. As she walked Jenna to the door, she said, "I would really like you to meet my husband before we make anything

official, but I would love to have you as our nanny."
Abra didn't realize it, but she lost Jenna after she said
the first part.

"I would love to meet your husband, too," she
responded. "I'll call you later to set something up,"
Abra said as she showed Jenna to the door.

That evening, Abra was working on making a
salad for dinner when Blaine came home from work.
"Hey Hon, how was your day?" Abra greeted him
cheerfully. Blaine walked over and gave his wife a kiss.

"It was fine. We only had three calls all day." He
went over to give Norah and Ellie a hug and kiss. "How
was the nanny hunt?"

"It went great! I really think I found one that
would be perfect." Abra tossed the lettuce in a large
bowl and began slicing tomatoes.

"You mean you found someone better than
Marsh?" he responded sarcastically.

Abra rolled her eyes and ignored his comment.
"Her name's Jenna. She's so good with the girls and
she's really easy to talk to. The girls absolutely loved
her! Norah was getting fussy at one point and she
picked her up and she cheered up right away and started
giggling." Blaine grabbed a knife and started helping by

cutting cucumbers for the salad. Abra grabbed the salad dressing out of the fridge and carried it over to the table. "I think you should probably meet her, and if you like her I think I'm going to give her the job." She dished out the salad on their plates.

"Maybe we can have her over tomorrow night for dinner," he suggested.

"Great. I'll give her a call later tonight and see if she's free."

That night, Abra finished cleaning the girls up from dinner and brought them into the living room to play while she made the call. "Hey Jenna, it's Abra. Just wanted to let you know that Blaine is really looking forward to meeting you." Jenna's heart fluttered at the thought of Blaine being excited to see her. Then she remembered he didn't know her.

Jenna needed some inspiration for new photos so she decided to head to a nearby city, Manteo, to take a break from beach pictures and capture some of the magnificent flowers and plant life at the Elizabethan Gardens.

"That's fantastic! I can't wait to meet him, Jenna responded."

"How about tomorrow? Would you like to come over for dinner?"

"Sure, what time?" It was silent on the other end while Abra thought it through.

"How about six?"

"That works for me. I'll see you then." Jenna had been walking without paying attention to where she was going. When she finally came back to reality, she saw she was standing in front of a short pathway. She walked down it, and at the end, it opened up to a beautiful fountain surrounded by bushes that were cut into the shape of diamonds. Jenna was astonished by the beauty. It would be the perfect place to have a wedding...her wedding.

The following day, Abra called some of Jenna's references. She called three different people; they all seemed to adore Jenna. What Abra didn't know was that at the end of each of those calls was the same Redhead, seeking revenge.

That evening, Blaine and Abra wandered around the kitchen making sure dinner turned out just right. Abra was very anxious for Blaine to meet Jenna. She hoped he would like her as much as she had. They decided to make eggplant parmesan, garlic bread, and salad for dinner. They had thought about doing fish or chicken, and then realized they didn't know if Jenna was a vegetarian or not. Blaine worked on the tomato sauce while Abra dipped the eggplant in egg and coated them in breadcrumbs. All of a sudden, Abra froze, egg and breadcrumbs pasted to her hands. "What if she's vegan?" she asked, concerned.

"Well, I guess she's stuck with salad," he said, laughing.

Abra cocked her head to the side, giving him an annoyed look. "That's not very nice." "Relax. I'm sure she's not," he reassured her.

When the doorbell rang, Ellie ran over to answer it. She stretched as far as she could, but the doorknob was just out of reach. Abra wiped her hands off on a dish towel and jogged to the door. She picked Ellie up and opened the door to let Jenna in. "Come on in. We're just putting dinner in the oven, so it'll be a little while."

Abra brought Jenna into the kitchen to introduce her to Blaine. This was the moment Jenna had been waiting for since she saw the advertisement in the paper. No, not since the advertisement--before that. The obsession had started long before that. It had been that first day she had laid eyes on him all those years ago. As Abra and Jenna rounded the corner, Jenna's heart pounded in her chest. The whole world seemed to be moving in slow motion.

"Blaine, this is Jenna," Abra said with a sweep of her hand. Blaine turned around from the stove. "Jenna, this is my husband, Blaine." Jenna and Blaine both froze in their tracks. Blaine was as gorgeous as Jenna had remembered. His dark hair and baby blue eyes gave him the boyish look she had always adored about him.

Jenna's heart was pounding. What if he remembered her? This thought had crossed her mind many times, but she ignored them. It had been so many years ago. She was a completely different person now. Almost one hundred and fifty pounds lighter, and thanks to her dermatologist, acne was no longer a problem. There was no way he would be able to recognize her. That didn't stop her stomach from doing somersaults, or her heart from beating so fast Jenna was convinced it had been visible to everyone around.

Blaine gave Jenna a suspicious look. There was something oddly familiar about Jenna, but he couldn't place it. He could have sworn he had seen her before.

"Nice to meet you, Jenna." he said, extending his hand. Jenna tried to hide her dreamy smile as she took his hand in hers. Jenna was relieved that Blaine hadn't paid any attention to the fact that she held onto his hand slightly longer than he did hers. Blaine shrugged. He didn't know anyone with that name. If they had known each other, surely she would have recognized him, but from her expression, she didn't recognize him at all.

Jenna let out a sigh of relief. She hadn't even realized she had been holding her breath the whole time. It was a smart idea changing her name. There was no way he would catch on if he hadn't already. He wouldn't see any reason why she would change her name. She knew she was not the same person she used to be. That fat dweeb was gone. This new woman was someone Blaine could actually fall in love with.

Abra finished setting the table while Blaine brought over the eggplant parmesan, garlic bread, and salad. "I must say, Abra is really excited about having you as our nanny," Blaine said, taking the spatula and trying to cut through the thick, stringy layer of cheese blanketing the eggplant. Being polite to their guest, he held his hand out for Jenna's plate first. He plopped a large piece of eggplant on her plate, cutting the lingering cheese with the edge of the spatula. She thanked him, giving him a smile and hovering the plate in the air for an extra couple of seconds.

"I know it can't be easy hiring someone you don't know, but I can assure you I will treat your daughters as if they were my own. I am really looking forward to getting started." She flashed Blaine another smile.

"Do you have any children?" Blaine asked.

"Not yet, but I would like to. I just never had the right guy."

"Oh, are you seeing someone now?"

"I have my eyes on someone, but nothing's come of it yet." She looked right into his eyes as she said it. There was a long, awkward silence before Blaine changed the subject.

"So, Jenna, what do you like to do in your free time?"

"I love scrapbooking and photography," Jenna said, hiding a sly grin. "How about you?"

"I love boating and playing just about any sport. Abra loves collecting seashells. She makes really nice crafts out of them. I keep telling her she should sell them, but she hasn't done anything with them yet. She'll have to show you sometime."

"Oh? What kinds of things do you make?" Jenna asked, turning towards Abra.

"I've done a few table tops, end tables and coffee tables, picture frames, mirrors..." Abra trailed off.

"I'd like to see your work sometime," Jenna said.

"Sure, I'd love to show them to you."

When they had all finished eating, Abra took Ellie and Norah to the bathroom to get them cleaned up and ready for bed.

"Did you want some help?" Jenna offered.

"Oh no, don't worry about it. This is my special bonding time with the girls," she said.

"Don't bother. I can't count the amount of times I've tried to give her a hand," Blaine teased. "This is Abra's time with the girls. You know, because she doesn't have enough time with them after being with them all day." Abra rolled her eyes at the mockery, but it was true. There was nothing Abra loved more than getting the girls ready for bed and reading them a bedtime story. Abra walked over and gave Blaine a kiss.

"I'll just be a couple of minutes," she said, carrying the girls downstairs to the bathroom.

"I'll clean up here!" Jenna hollered towards the steps. She grabbed the three plates and walked them over to the sink.

"So where did you grow up originally?" Jenna asked Blaine, trying to play along as she scraped the leftover tomato sauce into the trash, rinsed the plates, and put them in the dishwasher.

"I grew up not too far from here." Blaine looked for a glimmer of recognition in Jenna's eyes. There was nothing. "I moved to Ohio after high school to go to college. That's where I met Abra."

"Oh yeah? What made you decide to move back?"

"I always knew I wanted to move back here after school. I absolutely love the ocean and the beach. Now that the girls are a little older, Abra decided she wanted to go back to work, and she decided she was finally ready to move down here. How about you?"

Maybe this would help him figure out how he knew her. "I've lived here all of my life. You couldn't pay me enough to move away. I guess we have that whole ocean thing in common. You try to leave, but it's like a gravitational force that keeps pulling you back. Just like a magnet."

"You got that right."

"Have you ever climbed Cape Hatteras Lighthouse? Such an amazing view."

"When I was really young I did, but not recently." Blaine chuckled, "Abra would never in a million years climb up there. She's terrified of heights."

"Hmmm...interesting," Jenna commented.

"You said you've lived here all your life?

"Yeah, why?"

"You just look really familiar." Jenna started choking on her water.

"You ok?" Blaine asked.

"Yeah, sorry." She grabbed a nearby napkin and wiped her mouth. "I don't know why I would look familiar," Jenna said quickly.

Blaine shrugged, "maybe you just look like someone else I know."

"I guess I just have one of those faces," she smiled awkwardly.

"Oh well," he said, and moved on.

Abra bathed the girls and read them their bedtime story and then headed back to the living room to join Jenna and Blaine. The three chatted for a while and then Jenna took out her cell phone to check on the time.

"I better get going," she said as she stood up. Blaine and Abra followed suit. "It was great meeting you," Jenna told Blaine. Jenna leaned in for a hug, while Blaine went to shake her hand, putting them in an uncomfortable situation.

"Thanks again for dinner. It was delicious. I really hope you choose me as your nanny."

"No problem. I'll call you in the next couple of days to let you know for sure about the job. Have a safe drive. Talk to you soon." Abra said. They waved goodbye.

Once they closed the door Abra stared at Blaine, waiting for his opinion. "Well, what did you think?" She asked anxiously.

"I think if you like her we should hire her. Is there something familiar about her to you?" he asked.

Abra thought for a minute. "No, I don't recognize her at all. Maybe you've transported her before."

"Hmm...I don't know. I coulda sworn I've seen her somewhere before."

"She's not another one of your crazy patients, is she?" Abra asked, concerned. Blaine chuckled and quickly dismissed the idea.

Chapter 5

The sun shone brightly as Abra pushed Norah and Ellie in a double stroller down a sidewalk by their house. A refreshing salty breeze whipped through, cooling Abra and calming Ellie and Norah. As they strolled through town, Abra's mind soon began to wander. She thought about how excited she was to start her new job. She began to think about how she was going to decorate her classroom and what activities to do to get the kids acquainted with one another. Kindergarten was Abra's favorite year in school, which was why she was so happy that Nags Head had an opening for that grade. Kindergarten could be a scary and exciting year for young kids. It's the year when kids learn to read and write. Kids that age are so easily amused. When they finally finish reading their first book, it's like magic. Abra began to wonder when those magical moments disappeared. The older people get, the more it takes to impress them. Abra recalled that past Christmas, buying Ellie the coolest new toy. She knew Ellie would absolutely love it. When she tore open the paper Blaine took the toy out of the box. Ellie grabbed the box and started playing with it, not giving the toy a second thought. "We should have just given her a box," Blaine responded, laughing and shaking his head. Young kids are completely enthralled by that empty box. The older that same child gets, however, the harder it gets to please them. On Christmas morning, if they don't get the toy that has been sold out for months, they'll just die. Then it slowly gets worse. It then becomes, "I need this TV or the latest electronic device or car." Abra peeked at her girls in their stroller and wished they could stay at those ages forever.

Abra was so deep in thought that she almost didn't hear someone calling after her. Abra snapped back to reality.

"Oh, Sorry, Jenna, I was in another world."

"Don't worry about it. I was just out for a jog, and I saw you," Jenna said, out of breath. Abra assumed as much by looking at her. She was wearing an exercise top, spandex shorts and an iPod attached to an armband.

"I was actually planning on calling you this afternoon. Blaine and I talked it over and we would love to have you as our nanny," Abra said excitedly.

Jenna jumped up and down. "Really? Thank you so much!" She paused for a minute. What are you girls up to today? If you don't have any plans, would you want to grab something to drink? It's boiling out here." Jenna started fanning herself.

"Sure, that would be great. It's twice as hot in our house, so we decided to get out and hopefully find some air conditioning somewhere. We really need to cool off. Where do you want to go? I'm not too familiar with the area yet, so I'm still learning where the good places are to go."

"There's a Tropical Smoothie Cafe not too far from here. They have the best smoothies."

"I'll follow you," Abra responded. "Do you go jogging every morning?" she asked as they made their way to the cafe.

"Yeah, I try to jog a couple of miles every day."

"Wow, I wish I could do that," Abra commented.

"It's not so bad when you have a gym like this," Jenna gestured to the mesmerizing oceanic scene before them.

It didn't take long for everyone to cool off once they sat down in the cafe with their smoothies. Abra reached into the stroller and pulled out Ellie's Sippy cup to give to her. Then she pulled out Norah's bottle.

"So Blaine said he grew up here. Did you grow up around here too?" Jenna asked.

"No, I grew up in Ohio, near Cleveland. My family still lives there."

"Have they been down to see your house yet?" Jenna wondered.

"No, and they won't be down anytime soon."

"Oh? Why's that?"

"I haven't really spoken to my family in years. My parents didn't exactly approve of Blaine."

"What? Why not?" Jenna was outraged at the thought that someone didn't like Blaine. She quickly tried to control herself. "He seems like a great guy."

"Well, my family is Jewish. My first name, Abra, is the female version of Abraham. My maiden name is actually Schultz. So, as you can probably imagine, growing up, my parents always expected my sister and I to marry Jewish men. They were not too pleased when they found out that Blaine grew up Catholic. When my dad found out I was dating a gentile, he flipped out. Blaine and I dated for a year before we decided to get married. I had gone to Mass with Blaine quite a few times over that year and decided that I believed and wanted to live by the Catholic ways. Blaine and I had a long discussion about it and I decided that I wanted to convert to Catholicism. I remember the night I told my family I was going to trade in my Menorah for a Nativity Scene." Abra trailed off. "That was the night I told my parents Blaine and I were planning on getting married in a Catholic Church. I asked my parents if Blaine could come over for dinner. My father wasn't too happy about it, but my mom convinced him that it wouldn't hurt to have a guest over for dinner. HA! Boy was she wrong. I think I would have done less harm if I had taken a steak knife and stabbed my father in the back. When Blaine came over for dinner, we told him about me wanting to convert to Catholicism. He was furious. He stood up and started shaking his fist at Blaine, saying he had brainwashed me to leave my family roots, and if I gave up Judaism, I could kiss my family goodbye."

Jenna was sitting with her elbows on the table with her head resting in her hands. She was staring intently at Abra, waiting for her to finish the story. "What happened next?" She asked.

Abra shook her head. "I went back in the house, and my dad was in a horrible mood. He stomped around like there was cement in his shoes, slamming cupboards and doors. Later that night I was lying in bed, and my dad came in. He stood just inside the door, but talked as if I were a mile away. 'Young lady, I don't want you seeing that boy anymore!'" Abra did her best impression of her father. "I sat straight up in my bed. I told him that was going to be kinda hard and flashed my hand at him. He told me I was way too young to get married. I told him that we loved each other and we were getting married. He told me if I was mature enough to change my religion and get married I had to start acting like it. He then went on to tell me I had to move out." Abra paused. "So I packed my bags and left in the middle of the night." Abra looked up at Jenna. "I went to Blaine's that night. That was the last time I've seen my family. My parents haven't spoken to me since."

Abra set the straw wrapper down, causing it to spring up like a jack in the box. She took a long sip of her smoothie, trying to fight back the tears stinging her eyes. This was the first time Abra had spoken about her family since their falling out. What was it about Jenna that made Abra want to spill her guts? Maybe it was the fact that she hadn't really had a decent adult conversation with anyone other than Blaine since Ellie was born. Her girls kept her so busy she didn't make it out of the house much.

"That must be really hard on you," Jenna placed her hand on Abra's sympathetically.

"What's even harder is the fact that I haven't had any contact with Sadie since then. We were best friends growing up, but after I left, I never heard from her." Abra couldn't hold it back any more. The flood gates opened and couldn't be stopped. She began sobbing uncontrollably. "I apologize for getting so emotional. I guess I'm still not over it." She grabbed her napkin and dabbed at her eyes.

"Oh, don't worry about it. That's not something you can just get over. Does your sister feel as strongly as your parents?"

Abra took a deep breath and tried to pull herself back together. "No, not at all. She's just afraid of my dad. On the morning of the wedding, I received a phone call. I was busy getting ready and didn't get to the phone in time, but it was her number on the caller ID."

"You should really try calling her. Maybe she's afraid to call you." Jenna replied.

Abra thought about that for a minute. Sadie was the last one to call. Maybe Sadie had been trying to make things right, but Abra never gave her the chance.

Abra tried to change the topic by asking Jenna questions about herself, but as soon as she did, Jenna looked at her watch, "You know what, I didn't realize how late it was getting."

Abra looked down at the time, "I need to get going too. I have to get the girls back and fed. I found a gym nearby that offers kickboxing classes, so I wanted to try it out tonight."

Jenna raised her eyebrows. "I didn't know you did kickboxing."

Abra looked down at her body and made a face. "I used to years ago. It's a great workout. I want to get in shape so I thought I would check it out. You wanna join me?"

Jenna thought about it for a second. "Sure, why not? Just text me the time and place and I'll meet you there."

"Great! You never know, maybe there'll be some good-looking guys working out there too," Abra said, playfully jabbing Jenna in the arm.

"I actually have someone in mind," Jenna responded.

Abra gave her a quizzical look. "Spill!"

"Not right now. We can talk about it later. I have to run to the grocery store and pick some stuff up for dinner."

Abra was disappointed, but agreed. "I'll see you tonight," she said, giving Jenna a hug. Jenna realized she would have to suck up and be nice to Abra if she were going to keep her job as a nanny so she would become closer to Blaine.

Abra tossed her Styrofoam cup in the trash, gathered the girls, and headed out the door. The humid, sticky air instantly caused perspiration on Abra's face when she stepped out of Tropical Smoothie Cafe. While Abra was pushing the stroller home, she realized Jenna didn't really like to talk about herself. Whenever the conversation would get back to her, she would either change the subject or would come up with an excuse to leave. Abra shrugged it off, not giving it a second thought.

As Jenna strolled down the isles of the local Food Lion trying to find something to make for dinner, she realized she would have to be on her best behavior if she was going to get closer to Blaine. This was a job she could not be fired from. Unlike the fast food restaurant she worked at in high school. She wouldn't put up with crap from the customers, and, according to her boss at the time, it was inappropriate to flip off a customer when he got in her face and complained because Jenna got his order wrong. In Jenna's opinion, it was a mistake, let it go. It wasn't Jenna's fault anyway. Somebody distracted her when she was taking orders. She never heard them say no onions. Big deal. Pop in a stick of gum and move on. That's why she decided to do freelance photography. She had had two jobs since high school, not including her current job. After she was fired for flipping the guy off, she was hired to clean rooms at a hotel. She thought that would suit her better because she wouldn't have to deal with stupid morons all of the time. After having to clean up a room of vomit, condoms and other disgusting stuff, she realized that was worse than dealing with stupid people.

One day after work, she ran into one of her favorite teachers in the grocery store. It was her high school art teacher. When she asked Jenna what she had been up to, Jenna started to sound off about how awful her job was. The teacher told her she had always had vision and was very creative. She told Jenna she had wondered why Jenna never went into art or photography. Jenna gave it some serious thought, and that next week she took her final paycheck and went and bought camera equipment. Since then, she had various photos published in magazines, mostly ones that advertise vacationing at the Outer Banks. Her work was also shown all over the Outer Banks in the various art galleries, which she was very proud of.

At seven o'clock that night, Abra and Jenna met in front of the gym. They went inside and filled out papers at the front desk to become members. The lady then directed them to the room where they held the kickboxing class. As they were walking back, Jenna noticed a man lifting weights off to the side. He looked over and winked at her. Jenna was repulsed by him, but then she was struck by an idea.

When they reached the room, Jenna took a look around at all the people bent in every which way, stretching before the workout. "I think I'm just gonna hop on the elliptical out there. I'll meet you after class."

"What? No, you should stay," Abra grabbed her hand and started to pull her.

"No, it's okay. It looks really crowded. Don't worry. I'll just catch up with you after class." 80's rock music started blaring through the speakers. Abra shrugged and ran to find an empty spot.

Jenna walked over to the man that just winked at her. He was now wiping down his weights. Jenna leaned on the machine next to him. "Decided against the class? What? Was it too intense for you?" he teased.

Jenna flashed him the most flirtatious smile she could conjure up. "No, it wasn't too intense. I was just so distracted by watching you lift those heavy weights that I could barely concentrate on my kicks."

The man tossed his rag on the weights. "I usually lift twice this much, but I had a long...hard workout earlier, so I'm a little worn out now." Jenna laughed out loud and tried to cover it up with a cough. He extended his chubby, sweaty hand. "I'm Ron, by the way." Jenna cringed as she shook his hand. She hoped he hadn't noticed her wiping the sweat off on her leg.

"Hi, Ron, I'm...Abra," she said. Saying the name left a bad taste in her mouth.

"What a great name. What does it mean?" Ron asked.

"No idea," Jenna dismissed quickly. "So, Ron, would you like to meet for a drink sometime?" Jenna asked.

"Sure, how about tonight?"

"Now doesn't really work for me. How about if I give you my number and you can give me a call later?" Jenna and Ron both reached for their phones. Jenna scanned through her contact list. Ron gave her a curious look. "It's a new phone, I don't have the number memorized yet," she giggled and flashed her flirty smile again. Ron nodded in understanding. She rattled off the number and snapped her phone shut.

"Thanks," Ron said, raising his eyebrows at her, "I'll give you a call tomorrow night."

"Talk to you then." She turned and shook her butt as she made her way to the elliptical. Ron walked out shortly after, shooting her one last wink before he walked out the door. Jenna cringed and pedaled faster.

"Jab, cross, hook, uppercut!" the instructor hollered out. Abra was sweating bullets as she tried to stay on track. Following the instructor, Abra jumped, turned, and did the same thing with her left side. "AGAIN!" the lady shouted. When the song was over, the lady told everyone to get water. Abra, very conscious of every muscle in her body, dragged herself over to the sideline, grabbed a rag and wiped her face and took a long drink.

Standing beside her were two middle-aged women. One had blond hair, the other dark. "Hi! I'm Sandy, and this is Maria," the blond lady said.

"Don't stop moving!" the instructor hollered.

Abra picked up her feet and marched in place. "Nice to meet you. I'm Abra." Abra was going to say something else, but the instructor started hollering, "Come on back!"

"We'll catch up after class!" Sandy said.

The instructor switched song tracks and played *Girls Just Wanna Have Fun*. "Ok, let's do some X jacks." Abra was afraid to ask what those were. The lady started to do a jumping jack, but instead of a normal jumping jack, she jumped in the air, extending her legs into a split. Abra's mouth dropped. *Are you kidding me?* she said to herself, but still attempted. "Just one million more!" the instructor joked.

Abra's body felt like she was carrying a bag full of bricks as she pulled herself out of the room after class to find Jenna.

"Abra, hold up!" Sandy called after her. Abra waited for her and Maria to catch up.

"So how long have you been doing this?" Abra asked.

"I've been coming to this class for a couple of years. I dragged Maria here a couple of months ago and now she's hooked."

Maria smiled sheepishly. "It's true. She sucked me in. So will we see you again next week?" Maria asked.

"If I can move by then," Abra joked. Just then she saw Jenna. "It was really nice meeting you both. I'll definitely try to come next week." Abra said quickly and hurried towards Jenna.

"Great! Catch ya then," Sandy said.

Abra hurried over to Jenna. "How was your workout?" she asked. Jenna took a drink of water from her water bottle. She thought back to who guy that was going to call Blaine's phone, looking for Abra. "It was really good. How was the class?"

"Ugh, I realized just how out of shape I am."
Abra sighed. Jenna started laughing. They headed out
the door and parted ways.

Later that night, when Abra and Blaine were in
bed, Abra kept running through her and Jenna's
conversation from earlier that day in the café. Abra bit
her lower lip. "Blaine, do you think I should contact
Sadie?" Blaine let out a deep sigh. They'd had this
conversation constantly over the past couple of years.

"I dunno, Babe. She has had plenty of
opportunities to get a hold of you and she hasn't."

"But we moved," Abra interjected.

"Yeah, but you still have the same cell phone
number and e-mail. There's no way she couldn't get a
hold of you if she really wanted to."

"I guess you're right. I was talking about it with
Jenna today and she thinks it would be a good idea if I
contacted her. After all, she did try to call me when we
got married."

Blaine looked at her, "She did?"

Abra covered her mouth. Things had been so
stressful for the two of them when they got married that
she thought it would be better if she didn't mention

anything to Blaine about Sadie calling. "I saw the missed call when I was getting ready." Abra bit her lip.

"Did you ever think she was trying one last time to talk you out of marrying me before it was too late?"

That thought had never crossed her mind. "I'm just saying, if I want anything to change between us, I have to be the one to make the first move."

"Well, you're not going to do anything about it tonight. Why don't you sleep on it and see how you feel about it in the morning?" Abra nodded, leaning over to turn off the light. She curled up on her side and ran through it all over and over in her mind.

Chapter 6

Abra was rummaging through boxes and putting things away when she came across a box that wasn't labeled. She opened it up and saw it was full of old photo albums. She took one out and opened it. She flipped through the album until she came across a photo of her and her sister. She thought again about what Jenna had said. Why hadn't she contacted Sadie? She grabbed her cell phone out of her pocket and stared at it for a minute. She wondered to herself if it would be easier to have this conversation through e-mail. This way she could really focus on what she wanted to say and could add or delete things before she actually sent it. With a phone call there was a lot of room for error and of course there were always the dreaded awkward silences. If she didn't get a response back, she could assume Sadie never got the e-mail. She decided to think about it a little more while she unpacked some more boxes, but found herself not being able to concentrate. She put the albums away, ran back to the desk, and turned on the computer. She logged into her e-mail and hit the COMPOSE button. The words seemed to flow out of her like a stream. Years of thoughts and emotions that had built up now wanted to explode out of her, but she decided she would keep it short and simple.

Sadie,

I know it's been a long time, but I find myself thinking and worrying about you more and more. I'm so sorry for the way things turned out between us. I would really like for you to meet your two nieces. They're growing fast, and it would be a shame for them not to have their aunt in their lives. I really hope to hear from you soon. There is so much I've been wanting to tell you. I would love to hear what crazy and amazing adventures you've been on and where your life has taken you. I hope all is well with you.

Abra sat back in her chair, remembering everything Sadie and she had been through. Sadie was always the wild one, sneaking out late at night and constantly dating the wrong guys. Growing up, Abra never would have thought that she herself would be the one shunned from the family. Abra would never forget one night when Sadie was eighteen and she was sixteen. Sadie had snuck out in the middle of the night and came strolling in at two in the morning after having too much to drink. Abra had always been a light sleeper, so when Sadie started messing with the locks, Abra heard it. Abra crept through the halls and quietly opened the door.

"Sadie! What in the world do you think you're doing?" Abra whispered in an authoritative tone. Sadie giggled and stumbled into the house. Abra helped maneuver her sister through the hallways until one of the lights came on, and they saw their father making his way towards them. "Don't say anything," Abra whispered.

"What's going on down here?" Their father asked, half asleep and slurring his words. Abra began to panic. She had no idea what she should tell her dad. She ended up telling him that she herself was the one who had been sneaking out to go to a party. That decision had cost Abra a week of being grounded. Even after everything that happened, she never regretted saving her big sister.

Abra placed her fingers on the keyboard preparing to type "You still owe me big time," but decided against it. She closed with "We miss you and really hope to see you soon. Love you lots! Your one and only sister." Underneath she wrote "P.S. We moved," and wrote out their new address.

She grabbed the mouse and slowly brought it up to the SEND button. She thought about it some more and dragged the mouse to the SAVE button and let the screen fade to the screen saver of her, Blaine, and the girls at the beach recently. She started heading back down, but when she hit the last step, she turned and ran back up to the computer and quickly hit SEND before she changed her mind.

Blaine was outside sitting on the deck when his cell phone started ringing.

"Hello?"

"Huh, hi, is Abra there?"

"Yeah...?" Blaine said slowly. "She's busy right now, can I take a message?"

"This is Ron from the gym. We were supposed to get a drink tonight. Who is this?" Ron asked.

"This is her husband."

"Oh, I didn't realize she was married." Ron was starting to sound a little nervous.

"Well, she is. I'm not sure how you got this number, Ron, but if you know what's best for you, you'll delete it and never call it again!" Blaine hung up the phone and stared at it so hard he could have burned a hole through it.

He marched up the stairs and stormed into the girls' room. Abra quickly raised her hand to quiet him and pointed to the two sleeping girls. "We need to talk," he said forcefully.

Abra was thrown off by Blaine's tone. Blaine had never been one to lose his temper very easily. He had never had that tone with Abra, and she had never seen him look so enraged. Abra made sure the girls were all tucked in for the night and slowly went out in the hall. She had no idea what was in store for her, but she knew it couldn't be good. Abra grabbed the baby monitor, closed the girls' door, and led him to the living room. "What's going on?" Abra asked apprehensively.

He tossed the phone in the air towards her. "I don't understand," Abra asked, perplexed.

"Who the hell is Ron, and why are you meeting him for drinks?" Blaine snapped.

Abra cocked her head to the side. "I have absolutely no idea what you're talking about," Abra said, becoming more lost every second.

"He just called for you. He said you knew each other from the gym and that you were supposed to meet him tonight for drinks. What's this all about, Abra?" Abra threw her hands up in the air.

"I honestly have no idea what you're talking about. I didn't talk to any guy last night at the gym."

"Then how did he get your number?"

"I really don't know. Maybe it's just one of my friends trying to play a joke on me or something." They both knew that wasn't true. Abra didn't know a lot of people on the Outer Banks yet, and the ones she did know would never act like that.

"I don't know what to say. I don't think I'm comfortable with you doing kickboxing anymore."

This infuriated Abra. Blaine had never been the jealous type. He had never had any issues with her working out or going out without him. "Baby, listen to me," Abra said, saying anything and everything to save herself. *But how do you save yourself when there's nothing to save yourself from?* "If I were actually cheating on you, or making dates to go have drinks with guys, why would I give him your number? It doesn't make any sense. If something was going on, don't you think I'd be a little more discrete about it?" Abra said, trying to reason.

Just then, Norah started screaming at the top of her lungs. It was a blood-curdling cry that was unfamiliar to Blaine and Abra. They both bolted towards the room. Abra picked her up and looked her over. That was the hardest part of having young kids: knowing something is wrong and them not being able to discover what it is. "What's wrong, Baby Girl?" Abra held her close and rocked her. She sang *Jesus Loves Me* and *The Itsy Bitsy Spider*, which always calmed her down, but she still screamed. "Don't you feel well?" Norah was pulling on her ear so hard it was the color of a beet.

"I think she has an ear infection," Blaine responded. As the night went on, they tried everything, but nothing seemed to be working. Blaine ran to the other room and got some baby Tylenol. "We'll give her this tonight. If she's not better in the morning, we'll take her to Dr. Robinson."

It was times like these that Abra loved having Blaine around. He always seemed to know what to do in the event of a crisis. "I have to work tomorrow and so do you. Jenna's gonna have to take her to the doctor's."

Abra hadn't thought of this. She felt terrible. She'd always been able to take her daughters to the doctor's when they were sick. Now, she had to depend on someone else. This gave Abra a sickening feeling in her stomach.

"It'll all be okay. Don't worry." With all the commotion, Blaine dropped the subject of the phone call. Abra was right. He felt ridiculous even thinking that Abra would do anything like cheat on him. She was an incredible wife and mother.

The next morning, Abra woke up and walked in the nursery. Ellie was sound asleep, but Norah was wide awake, her ear still dark red. Abra reached in and picked her up. "It's okay, Norah. Jenna's going to take you to the doctor's, and he'll make you all better." She gently stroked her head and held her close. She carried her up into the kitchen and started a pot of coffee. She heard Blaine moving around so she took out an extra coffee cup. Blaine came up shortly after. Abra handed over his coffee. "Do you think I should take the day off? Norah still isn't feeling well. I think I should be the one to take her to Dr. Robinson."

"She'll be fine, Abra, really. Plus, it's the first day of school. You can't call off today." He somewhat chuckled at the ridiculousness of the idea. "I know you want to be the one to take her, but you're a working woman now." Abra was already starting to second guess her decision to work.

When Jenna arrived, Abra explained about Norah being sick and that they gave her Tylenol the previous night. "I really hate doing this to you, and I hate the thought of leaving my daughter when she's sick." Abra felt like she was letting Norah down by leaving her when she was sick and needed her the most.

"I'll take great care of her." Jenna assured her. "You better hurry; you don't want to be late on your first day." Abra gave her girls one last kiss and left.

Jenna packed up both girls to take them to the pediatrician. She walked up to the front desk. Taking a child to the doctor was completely foreign to her. She tried not to think about all the germs floating around her. She could feel them crawling all over her as she signed Norah's name on the sign in sheet. Jenna stood in the waiting room with the girls for a half hour. She was starting to get impatient, when a nurse finally showed them to a room. Shortly after, Dr. Robinson, a very attractive man, not too much older than Jenna, walked into the room.

"Well, Hello," he said. Jenna recognized his tone. It was the same tone men used when they were trying to pick her up at a bar. Men were all the same in Jenna's eyes. They were all like dogs drooling all over themselves. All men except one. It did make Jenna wonder why her beauty seemed to work on every man except the one that actually mattered to her.

After asking what seemed like a million questions about Norah that Jenna couldn't answer, such as if she had been sleeping at night, or if she'd shown any other signs of being ill, Dr. Robinson prescribed Tylenol and told Jenna to bring Norah back if she wasn't feeling any better in three days.

"How long have you been the nanny?" He asked.

"Just started, actually. Today's my first day."

"Wow, they're really throwing you into the lion's den right off the bat. Just starting and already have a sick child." Jenna shrugged, "It's not that bad."

"It was really nice meeting you, Jenna. I hope to see you again sometime," he smiled.

"I hope not," Jenna attempted to joke.

He laughed, "Well, obviously not here. Maybe outside of the office sometime. Maybe for coffee or dinner."

"Sorry, I'm spoken for." Jenna said.

The doctor blushed, "Oh, I didn't realize. I just noticed you weren't wearing a ring."

"It's okay. Are we all done here?" She asked, trying to escape.

"Yeah, she should start to feel better soon."

"Thanks," Jenna said simply while she gathered the diaper bag and girls and left the office.

Right after the appointment, Jenna loaded the girls back into the car. She looked at them, and all of a sudden it hit her. She had never taken care of kids by herself. She had no idea where to begin. Even though it might not be her top choice, there was only one person she could think of that she could turn to. She stopped thinking and just drove. She had driven the same route so many times before, on her way home. At this point, she was confident she could make the drive with her eyes closed.

It wasn't long before Jenna stood in front of a big red wooden door with two screaming children. Maybe she had spoken too soon at Dr. Robinson's office when she said it wasn't so bad. A short, petite lady soon opened the door. "Laney? It's been a while," the lady greeted. Jenna cringed at the sound of her old name.

Laney and her mother, Janice, never had a close relationship. Laney's father had left the two of them when Laney was just a baby. As far back as she could remember, her mother had not had a single relationship that lasted longer than a month. By the age of five,

Laney became accustomed to the comings and goings of each of her mother's failed relationships. This carried through Laney's teenaged years. It became very common for Laney to come home to see her mother crying her eyes out over a half a bottle of wine and a heaping bowl of chocolate fudge ice cream. One day Laney had had enough of her mom and all of her boyfriends. Watching her mother stagger around the house carrying a box of tissues, watching sappy romantic movies, and waiting for Prince Charming to come take her away made Laney realize she never wanted to go through what her mother went through. Laney decided she would not go jumping from guy to guy and leave the minute she found something imperfect about him. Laney decided she was going to find her soul mate and hang on for dear life. The following day was when she finally came face-to-face with Blaine Ryan. Laney took it as a sign. Blaine was her soul mate.

"Hi, Janice," she finally responded. Janice, just now noticing the two kids, had a look of surprise and confusion on her face.

"I guess it's been longer than I thought," Janice responded.

"No, they're not mine. This is Ellie," she smoothed Ellie's hair with her hand, "and this is Norah. Can we come in?" Janice stepped aside and motioned her in.

"So who do these two beautiful girls belong to?" Janice asked, raising her voice a couple of octaves as she bent down to pick up Norah.

"Do you remember Blaine Ryan from high school?"

Janice nodded. Remember him? How could she forget? Janice spent months picking up the pieces left of her daughter and putting them back together. It was seven years ago. High school was a horrific time in Laney's life. She would come home almost every other day in tears because of things her classmates did or said. She remembered one time in particular. It was the summer before Laney started high school. Laney had always been on the heavier side. Over that summer, she had put on a lot of weight. Her whole freshman year it seemed like each and every one of her classmates took turns tormenting her about it. They were constantly calling her names and making comments. She'd get embarrassed and turn red, which caused the other kids to harass her more, calling her a red M&M. The name calling was bad enough, but there was one time in particular that hurt Laney beyond repair.

She had been standing in line at the grocery store, when the lady in front of her turned to her and looked down towards her stomach. "Aw, when are you due?" She had asked, rubbing Laney's belly. The head cheerleader was within ear shot and couldn't help but burst out laughing. Laney was completely mortified. She threw down what she was carrying and ran out the door. Before Laney even got home, it seemed word had spread to everyone at school. That whole next month, she was constantly tormented. The girls would stuff basketballs under their shirts and prance around during gym class.

That was when her life had been changed forever. Blaine had been walking down the hall, where a group of guys were surrounding Laney. Her face was red and swollen from crying. Blaine didn't really know the girl, but he couldn't stand by and watch a girl be tortured. He rushed over and pulled them away from her. This of course turned the attention to Blaine. The guys started making comments about Blaine being the father of the "baby." Laney knew Blaine, but who didn't know the school's star football player? Ever since that day he stood up for her, she had become completely infatuated with him. She had pictures of Blaine she had taken at football games posted all over her walls. She spent the remainder of her high school career chasing after him. She went to every football, baseball, and basketball game there was to support him. Laney never even paused to check out another guy. Laney was convinced that she and Blaine were meant to be together.

"Mom, are you listening?"

"I'm sorry, dear. What were you saying?"

"These are Blaine's daughters. I've been taking care of them."

"What about their mother?" Janice asked

"Well, that's why I am watching the girls." Jenna moved Norah to her other hip. She stopped and thought for a minute. "Since she had this bundle of joy," she bounced Norah again, "she's suffered with postpartum depression. She's constantly crying, and can barely get out of bed. She's not able to take care of the girls. It's really hard for Blaine to be around her anymore. He wants to be with me, but it just breaks his heart to see his wife suffering. He's planning on telling her he wants a divorce, but he's afraid of what she'll do to herself or the girls if he does."

The whole time Jenna was talking, Janice couldn't help but wonder how much of her daughter's story was true, if any. She went over and took a screaming Norah from Jenna. "What's wrong with this little one?" She said raising her voice an octave.

"She has an ear infection. This is the first time I've been alone with them, and I don't have a clue what I'm doing." Jenna said frantically.

"I'm so glad you came over. There's something I've been wanting to tell you for a couple of years now. Ever since you left." Janice trailed off.

"I'm only here because you're the only one I know who I thought could help me take care of these girls. Otherwise, I wouldn't be here."

"I don't care the reason. You're here and that's all that matters to me. There's something I've been wanting to tell you for three years now, but I haven't known how. You wouldn't take my calls. I started writing letters, but when I would read them back they just didn't do justice to how I truly felt. Laney, I am so sorry for what I've done to you. I'm sorry I always chose my boyfriends over you, and I'm very sorry for not believing you when you told me about Bob."

"What? Did he finally leave you?"

"No, I left him. Part of me knew you were telling me the truth, but I didn't want to believe it. So, I finally confronted him. He lied about it at first, but then when he was at work, I started snooping around in his stuff and I found his collection of child pornography. I called the cops, and he was arrested that evening."

"I'm glad you finally saw who he really is," Jenna said flatly.

"Laney, please forgive me. I know I've screwed everything up and made a mess out of both of our lives, but I'm really trying to change. I've even started going back to church."

"Why? Is the preacher hot?"

Janice was starting to get frustrated. "Look, I'm trying to apologize. Everyone makes mistakes, and the sooner you realize that, the easier your life will be."

"I forgive you for dumping me off at a different person's house every night so you could go out with whoever your boyfriend was at the time to go partying. I've made my peace with that. What I can't forgive you for is for calling me a liar when I told you about Bob. I knew you were a little ditzy, but you were still my mother. I thought I could trust you and come to you when I needed something."

"And you can," Janice interjected.

"Oh yeah? How many times did I tell you Bob had been touching me and doing things to me? Ten? Twenty? Yet every time you would call me a liar and send me to my room. The final time when he actually raped me, and I told you, you actually slapped me! That's when I knew I was on my own. I knew you couldn't be trusted and I would have to take matters into my own hands. That's when I left." Jenna stood up to leave. "I shouldn't have come here. I don't know why I would have thought we could have a normal, mother/daughter conversation."

"Please, don't leave again. I can't let you walk out of my life mad at me again."

"Tough," Jenna said and started to put Norah back in her carrier. "I'm sure I can do this on my own."

"Laney Michele Williams, you stay right here!"

This took Jenna by surprise. She couldn't remember the last time her mother used that tone and her full name with her. She felt like she was a kid again. She sat back down.

"I can't change the past, but I want to change the future. I want a future where you and I have a normal relationship. One where you can call me up and you can tell me all about everything that happened to you that day. One where I can help you whenever you have a problem and make your life easier, not harder, for once."

Jenna saw a side to Janice that she had never seen before. The one who was finally putting her daughter first. The honest and sober one. The person she had never seen before was a mother.

Janice knew there had to be something she could do to make up for all the wrong decisions she'd made as a mother. It was time she was the mother her daughter needed. She cuddled Norah while Laney tried to control Ellie, who kept wandering towards the nearby staircase that lead to the basement. Janice started singing softly a song that she had sung to her daughter when she was a baby. Soon after, Norah was fast asleep.

Jenna was amazed. "How did you do that?" She whispered.

"If you want, I would love to show you."

Jenna didn't know if it was the fact that she had finally forgiven her mother, or the fact that she was determined to figure out how to be a mom herself so she could win over Blaine, but she spent the rest of the day learning as much as she could about taking care of young kids. She had to get this right. She had to prove to Blaine that she would be a more suitable mother to his daughters than Abra.

Chapter 7

Abra had butterflies in her stomach as she stepped into what would feel like her new home for the next couple of months.

When the time finally came for the buses to arrive, it was pure chaos. The air smelled like diesel fuel burning. The parking brakes hissed, followed by the roaring of anxious students ready to start a new year. The kids came charging at her like it was Black Friday, and she was the cashier at Best Buy.

Abra stood in front of her desk hollering out to the young boys and girls that walked in to find the seat where their name tag was. She waited for all her students to get in their proper places. "Hello, everyone! My name is Mrs. Ryan," Abra announced, pointing towards her name written on the dry erase board behind her, "and I'll be your teacher for the the year." Abra had the class spend the morning working on craft projects and writing skills.

When lunchtime finally arrived, the students all lined up to get their lunches. Abra told everyone to grab their lunches and come back to their seats. Abra grabbed her lunch out of her desk drawer and started unpacking the contents. The kids all ate and chatted excitedly. All of a sudden they started panicking. "Mrs. Ryan, Mrs. Ryan! Something's wrong with Tommy!"

Abra ran over to the little boy who was gasping for air. "Tommy, what's wrong?" Abra said, trying to keep her voice calm and steady. "Tommy! Tommy! Say something!" Abra ordered. The young boy wheezed and was able to squeak something out, but Abra couldn't make out what it was. Abra pointed to a girl standing next to her and hollered, "Go to the office and get the nurse! Hurry!" Abra's cool, calm, and collected attitude had quickly dissipated. There were red splotches covering Tommy's face and neck, and he was panicking, flapping his arms, trying to communicate. Abra tried to calm him. "It'll be okay Tommy, don't worry. We're getting you help. Someone went to get the nurse. Everything's going to be okay."

The nurse rushed in not a minute later. "What's going on?" She said, running over to Abra.

"Tommy's having difficulty breathing."

"Tommy?" The nurse said urgently. She looked on his desk and picked up a peanut butter and jelly sandwich with a big bite bitten out of it. "Tommy, did you eat this?" The nurse asked. Tommy nodded. "Okay, we need to call 911 and get him help now!" the nurse yelled. Abra was still confused about what was going on. "Tommy has a bad nut allergy. He can't have peanut butter!" The nurse was trying to be as calm as she could.

Abra grabbed her cell phone and dialed 911. While she was on the phone, she saw the brown lunch bag on Tommy's desk. On the front in big black letters it read JOEY.

"He's allergic to peanut butter. He's going into anaphylactic shock. We need to get him to the hospital now! His airway is closing!"

Just then, Blaine ran in with a male and a female paramedic. Abra was relieved to see Blaine. Except for when Blaine had saved her, Abra had never seen Blaine in action. She was totally mesmerized by him. She was amazed at how he knew exactly what to do and was able to stay calm the whole time.

By the end of the day, Abra could barely move. *What have I gotten myself into? It's one thing to take*

*care of your own kids, but to be responsible for
someone else's is a completely different story.* Abra
walked in the door and collapsed on the couch.

Jenna came strolling in carrying Norah. "How
was your first day?" She asked joyfully.

Abra moaned.

"That good, huh?" Jenna replied.

"I had one kid who kept eating paste and
another who decided to cut the long corn silk hair of the
girl sitting in front of him," Abra said with more than a
hint of exhaustion in her voice.

"What a day," Jenna chuckled.

"That's not even the worst of it!" Abra started.
She told Jenna all about Tommy having to be taken to
the hospital.

"How awful! Is he going to be okay?" Jenna
asked sympathetically.

"Yeah. I guess they sent him home already, but
it was still traumatizing." Abra perked up when she saw
Ellie and Norah. "Plus, I missed my favorite girls like
crazy!" she exclaimed, reaching out for Norah. "How
was she today?" Abra asked.

"I think she's feeling a lot better. She seemed
more like herself this afternoon," Jenna told her. Abra

took a close look at Norah. The color was returning to her face, and her ears weren't as red. "I hope you're hungry. Dinner should be ready soon." Jenna announced.

Abra was very grateful to have Jenna around. The last thing she wanted to do after the long day she had was to have to worry about cooking dinner. Abra stood up and took a look around for the first time. The house was spotless. Not a single toy was out of place.

"If there's nothing else you need me to do I guess I'll get going," Jenna said.

"You're not staying for dinner? You made all this delicious food. You have to stay and enjoy it with us."

"Thanks, maybe another time. I'll see you tomorrow." Abra walked Jenna to the door.

That night at dinner, Blaine noticed Abra was really quiet. "You okay, Babe? You've barely touched your food."

Abra snapped back to reality. "I'm sorry. What did you say?"

"What's the matter?"

"I just can't get Tommy out of my mind."

"I'm glad everything turned out ok. I was worried about him when we dropped him off. He must be doing a lot better if they sent him home already." Abra nodded and tried to stomach some of her food. That was one thing about being a paramedic. Once you dropped a patient off at the hospital, you never heard any update or outcome. You never heard anything about that patient again.

Even though Abra knew Tommy was alright, she was so relieved when she saw him in school the next day. When Abra heard her boss, Kate, was looking for her in her office, she just wanted to go home and climb back into bed.

"Abra, have a seat."

Abra jumped in before Kate had the chance to start in on her. "Kate, I feel horrible about what happened to poor Tommy. I had no idea he picked up the wrong lunch. By the time I found out, it was too late."

"I'm sorry. I understand, Abra. Those things happen. It's very important that you know allergies and other special needs your students have."

"I understand. I'll be very careful from now on. I will personally hand out the lunches to everyone so we don't have that same problem again."

"That will be all. You should get back to class," Kate motioned her away with her wrist.

Some days at the station were very slow. They could go a whole shift without being dispatched out for anything. Blaine, Sam, and the rest of the afternoon crew sat around chatting for a couple of hours, when the shrill sound of the tones came over the loud speaker. "Attention all Fire Department personnel: report of a fully engulfed structure fire," the dispatcher called out. The men jumped up, threw on their gear, and hopped up into the truck.

"Here we go!" Sam called out behind the wheel. He flipped on the lights and sirens and flew down the road.

They finally arrived to the address they were dispatched to about seven minutes later, but that felt like an eternity when every minute could be the difference between life and death. There was an older lady standing on the front porch hollering at them as they got out of the truck.

"Save my baby! Save my baby!"

"We'll do our best ma'am, just stand back," Sam ordered as he and Blaine prepared to go inside. The combination of everything in a house that caught fire caused a mixture of nauseating and toxic smells as the firefighters placed their SCBA masks on. They crawled around inside the pitch blackness. Blaine went in first, and Sam crawled in behind him. They were crawling around when John heard a loud cracking ahead of him.

"Get out!" He yelled.

Blaine and Sam quickly turned and rushed out as quickly as they could. Right as they stepped outside, the house collapsed to the ground. It sounded like a bomb went off as the house crumbled down in flames.

Blaine looked over at the owner. She screamed out in horror as she saw her whole life go down in flames. This was the absolute worst part of the job in Blaine's eyes. He had no problem risking his life to save another, as much as Abra hated to hear that, but to watch the ones he wasn't able to help just tore him in half. He couldn't stand to watch the lady as she came to the realization that she was going to have to start her life over from scratch. Blaine had forgotten how difficult it was to watch people in pain. As he began to slowly walk over to the lady, trying to formulate what he was going to say, the scene commander grabbed his shoulder.

"Ryan, before you go say anything, I thought you should know that her 'baby' was her beloved Shih Tzu. Still sucks, but could have been a lot worse." Blaine nodded and continued over, telling the homeowner, "I am so sorry. I wish there was something more I could have done." The lady tried to pull herself together.

"I know you did everything you could have. Thank you." she said through her sobs.

Blaine went home that night, grateful and feeling unbelievably blessed for everything he had in his life.

"Blaine, is that you?" Abra called out when she heard the door open.

"Yeah, it's me," he said. He walked up to her and took her in his arms and squeezed her tightly for nearly five minutes.

"Did something happen?" She asked.

"I just had a bad call. Made me realize how lucky we are. I'll be okay. I just want you to know how much you and the girls mean to me. I don't know what I would do without you. You are the most amazing woman I've ever met."

Abra started to tear up. Normally, Blaine wasn't into the mushy, lovey-dovey stuff. She decided to savor the moment.

Chapter 8

That Friday morning, Kate walked into Abra's room as she was writing her lesson for the day on the dry-erase board before the kids arrived. "So how was your first week, besides the Tommy incident?" Kate asked as she leaned against Abra's desk. Just as Abra was about to open her mouth, Kate cut her off. "That's wonderful. So listen, we've started an after-school program where kids can stay for a couple of hours after school—to help out the parents who have to work late and don't have any place for their kids to go."

"That's a great idea. I'm sure that really helps a lot of parents out."

"It does. We have a lot of parents and students who have benefited from it. The problem is, Mrs. Simpson called off today, and she was one of our helpers, so we are short handed on teachers today. I was wondering if you could stay and take her place tonight?"

"Uhhm, well...I..."

"Great! We meet in the gym after the buses leave," Kate said before Abra had a chance to protest. Kate turned around quickly and took off out the door before Abra could say another word.

She mumbled profanities under her breath. She immediately stopped when her kids started walking in the class. Abra jumped up quickly and forced a smile on her face. After everyone was situated, she broke them up into reading groups.

During her lunch hour, Abra rocked back and forth in her swivel chair. She realized Blaine was on call at the station all night. She grabbed her cell phone out of her purse and called Jenna to tell her the change of plans.

"Hey, Jenna. I'm really sorry, but I'm going to be home late tonight. I was volunteered to help with an after-school program. Then I forgot I have a couple of errands I need to run after that. It'll probably be eight o'clock before I get home."

"That's not a problem. We'll see you when you get home."

"Okay, thanks. I hate to ask this of you, but if you could feed the girls dinner, I'd really appreciate it."

"Sure, that would be fine. I can even give them baths and put them to bed."

"No, you don't have to do that. I'll take care of that when I get home. They'll be fine to stay up a little later one night." Abra would hate to miss that time with the girls. Abra hung up the phone and ferociously tore into the sandwich she made for herself earlier that morning.

Jenna hung up and did a little dance. She was really starting to get attached to the girls. They were starting to feel like her own. She couldn't help but think that this is the life she could have had. It made her boil inside. Abra took this life from her, and it was about time Jenna started to fight for it. She wouldn't let it bother her right now. She had the whole day with the girls, and she planned on making the most of it. Her main goal was to make those girls fall in love with her so much that it made Abra feel so inferior that she realized Jenna was definitely the better fit for the family and left. That would not be an easy chore, but nothing had ever come easy for Jenna. Why should this be any different?

Jenna went online to try to find some ideas of what she could do with the girls all day. She finally came across something that she realized would be perfect.

Before long they arrived in the parking lot of Kitty Hawk Kites. Jenna looked over at Jockey's Ridge and saw a family on top of the hill riding horses. When they walked in, the array of colors and styles of kites had Ellie in complete awe. She jumped up and down and started running around, reaching for everything in sight. Jenna grabbed her right before she knocked something over. Norah was in a stroller trying to escape. Jenna was proud of herself. She knew they would love it.

Once they left Kitty Hawk Kites, they walked next door to the Outer Banks Bear Company. "What adorable girls!" the lady exclaimed when they walked in the door.

"Thank you. I wanted to get something special for my..." she paused for a quick second before she continued, "daughters."

"Of course. Why don't you pick out which pet pals you would like, and we'll get started."

"What do you think, Ellie?" Jenna asked. Ellie started tugging on a rabbit and a frog. "How about we make one of them for your sissy?" Ellie nodded. They put stuffing in the animals, and Jenna helped pick clothes for them to wear.

As they were finishing making the stuffed animals, Jenna realized it was Friday. That meant the weekend was coming. She hated the weekends, because it meant she would be away from her girls and Blaine for two days. It wasn't fair.

When they got home, Jenna took the kite that they bought out of the bag and put it together. Once the wind caught it and it was high up the girls started cheering and jumping up and down. It made Jenna smile to know that she made them happy.

After school, Abra met up with the other teachers involved in the program. Most of whom looked just as happy to be there as Abra did. She knew they had probably been suckered into it just like she had. Abra kept reminding herself that this was what she had signed up for when she decided to start working outside of the home. She didn't realize how hard it would be to be away from Ellie and Norah.

Abra walked over to one of the other first grade teachers, Emily Roberts, who was pouring fruit punch into cups for the kids. "Can I help you get the snacks ready, Emily?" Abra asked.

"Sure," Emily responded, unenthused.

Abra grabbed the bag of pretzels sitting on the table and poured them into the nearby bowl. "You sound as thrilled to be here as I am," Abra pointed out.

Emily gave her a stern look. "I'm missing my son's first soccer game right now."

Abra gave her a sympathetic look. "I'm sorry. I kind of know how you feel. This is my first time working outside the home since my daughters were born, and I'm having a tough time being away from them."

"I hated going back to work after my son was born, but I didn't really have a choice. Someone has to pay the bills." Emily said and called the kids over to get their snack.

Sam and the rest of the crew decided they all wanted to stop for a beer before heading home after their shift. They washed the soot and dirt off of their faces in the bathroom and headed to a nearby bar.

"You coming, Ryan?" One of the other guys asked.

"Oh, I dunno. I should probably get home, help Abra out with Norah and Ellie.."

"Isn't that what women are best at? Watching the kids? I mean, otherwise guys would be the ones carrying them for nine months," Sam said, laughing.

"The fact that you are not married truly astounds me," Blaine commented.

"I'm just sayin'," Sam said, walking away.

Blaine didn't want to tell the guys the real reason why he probably shouldn't go. He thought it would be better for his ego if he decided not to go on his own, rather than have his wife forbid him going out.

But eventually, Blaine gave into peer pressure and decided he would go with the guys and stay for one quick beer before heading home. Abra wouldn't have to know. He was once again the newbie in the department. He didn't want to be the one who never joined in. He decided he would call Abra when he was on his way home. You could never tell how long a fire call would be, so Abra would have no idea he went out.

They all got their beers and started drinking when a tall, blond lady walked up to the bar and started to order a drink.

Sam looked her up and down. "Why don't you put that on my tab?" Sam told the bartender. The bartender nodded. This particular bar was a common place for the firefighters to hang out.

The tall blond flashed Sam a brilliant smile. "Thanks..." she trailed off waiting for Sam to tell her his name.

"Sam," he responded, finishing her sentence.

"Did you guys get all fancied up just for me?" She asked as she looked at their dirty t-shirts and disheveled hair.

"My buddies here and I are firemen. Blaine looked at his watch. "It only took thirty seconds to drop the F bomb. Watch her fawn over him," Blaine said to one of the other firemen.

"We just got off of a call," Sam continued.

The lady's eyes lit up. "Oh, you're a firemen? Wow, that has to be such a rewarding job," she said in awe.

"It really is. Just the gratitude shown by the community is payment enough for what we do," Sam said placing his hand over his heart for emphasis.

"In my opinion, you don't get paid enough," the lady said.

A couple of minutes had passed, and Sam finally said, "Hey, guys, Bethany and I are going to get out of here."

"Catch ya later," Blaine said, not surprised at all. Sam had always been a ladies' man. Blaine was shocked at how quickly he was able to get a ladies' phone number. He was so grateful to have Abra. He would hate to be in the dating pool again.

After Sam and the lady, apparently named Bethany, had left, Blaine turned his chair towards John, one of the other guys on the department. He had started a couple months after Blaine had left, so Blaine didn't really know him too well. Blaine shook his head towards John, "Some things never change."

"Tell me about it." John reached in his pocket and pulled out his wedding ring to put it back on. They weren't allowed to wear any form of jewelry when they responded to a call.

"So you're married?" Blaine asked, excited to not be surrounded by singletons.

"Yep, I've been married for seven wonderful years. We have three kids." He took out his phone and pulled up the pictures of two girls and a baby boy.

Blaine smiled, "Cute kids."

"How about you?" John asked back.

"Yeah, I'm married. I just left my ring on the dresser so I wouldn't lose it." Blaine took out his phone and shared the pictures of Abra, Norah, and Ellie.

"Beautiful family," John responded. "So how does it feel to be back on the department after being gone so long?"

"It's taking a little adjusting to. It's definitely different being back now that I have a family to think about. I'm sure my wife would be thrilled if I could find a different job that isn't so dangerous, but this is who I am. I think she understands that. It's also a little bizarre how some people were here when I was on the department before, yet there are quite a few people that started after I left, like you, yet you have higher seniority. I feel a little stuck in the middle." Blaine finished his beer. "I better get going home," he said waving for the bartender to get him his bill.

"Yeah, me too. I'll walk out with you," John said.

"I wonder how Sam made out with Bethany," Blaine commented, chuckling, as they walked to their vehicles.

"Same old, I imagine. He'll sleep with her, then tomorrow he'll tell her he's too emotionally damaged to commit to anyone. Then the next time we go out, he'll do the same exact thing," John said, shaking his head. He hopped up into his Ford F150. He rolled down the window. "Nice talking with you, Ryan. Catch ya later," and he drove off.

"Hello? Anyone home?" Abra called out cheerfully as she walked into the house. She closed the door behind her, took a look at the clock, and was disheartened. It was already past 8 o'clock. She hung the keys on the hook hanging beside the door and tossed her purse on the table. It had been an extremely long first week, but it was now the weekend, and she planned on spending every single moment with her two favorite little ladies and her husband. This thought immediately picked up her mood.

She glided along the wooden floors as if she were floating in midair. She blissfully made her way up the stairs, lightly tapping a happy tune on the banister. She peaked in Ellie and Norah's bedroom and stopped dead in her tracks. Looking in the room, she saw Jenna, with Norah on her one side and Ellie on the other. Ellie and Norah were both in their pajamas, clearly having just got out of the bath. Norah was fast asleep. Ellie laid there with her head on Jenna's chest. Jenna had Ellie's favorite book in hand, "Are You My Mother?" Abra did not appreciate the irony. She was infuriated that she missed her daughters' and her nighttime ritual.

Ellie pointed excitedly at the page and looked up adoringly at Jenna. It felt like a dagger in Abra's heart. For the past two years, Abra never missed bathing her girls, getting them in their pajamas, and reading them a bedtime story. It was such a special routine they had every night. Had she known that this job would sacrifice so much of her time with her daughters, she wouldn't have taken it.

Hearing Jenna read the words to her daughters was sickening to Abra. Being that it was Ellie's favorite book, Abra had read the story out loud a million times, but it never affected her the way it did at this very moment. As Jenna read about the little bird traveling all over searching for its mother, Abra grew panicked and hoped that didn't happen with her daughters.

Just then, Jenna looked up. "I didn't hear you come in," she said softly. She then looked back down at Ellie and Norah and tried to hide the vicious smile on her face. "I know you said to wait, but I could tell they were getting really tired."

It took all Abra had to be able to choke out "That's okay," all the while thinking, *you don't know my daughters at all!* "Well, I'm home, so you don't have to stick around." Abra could tell it came out a lot harsher than she had anticipated. "I'm sorry. I didn't mean it like that."

Jenna shrugged it off. "It's okay." She held the girls close. "Goodnight, my favorite little girls. I'll see you both in a couple of days." She placed the girls gently in their beds, flashed a smile at Abra, and headed out the door.

Abra wasn't sure if it was all in her head, but she couldn't help but think that Jenna was doing this on purpose to make her feel bad. Jenna knew how much putting her daughters to bed at night meant to her, yet she did it anyway.

Chapter 9

Abra was so excited when she woke up Saturday morning she practically jumped on the bed to wake Blaine up. She felt like a five-year-old on Christmas morning. She did some things around the house until Ellie and Norah woke up.

Abra put them in the living room and had them play with their stuffed animals from Jenna. Blaine, still not fully awake, walked in shortly after.

"Coffee?" Abra asked, chipper.

"Yes, please," he said sleepily. He walked in the living room to play with the girls while he waited for his coffee to finish brewing.

"Where did these come from?" Blaine asked, taking the stuffed animal Ellie was lying with.

"Jenna took the girls to Outer Banks Bear Company yesterday."

"That was nice of her. I guess it's about time Ellie put down that old raggedy doll."

Abra whipped around, grabbed the frog out of Blaine's hands and threw it down.

"She does NOT need something new. There is absolutely nothing wrong with Heidi. She loves Heidi. You know as well as I do that she never goes anywhere without her!" Abra said, crescendoing to a shout.

Blaine surrendered. "Okay, sorry. I didn't realize *Ellie* needed her so much." He gave her a sly smile.

"Well, she does." Abra humphed and left the room to change into her swimsuit for the beach that day.

Once everyone was in their swimsuits and had sun block on, they walked down to the beach. In that moment, sitting on the blanket with her family, happy and healthy, there was nowhere else in the world Abra would have rather been. Abra brought buckets down with them so they could make sand castles. Ellie jetted toward the water.

"Hold on, little fishy," Blaine said as he scooped her up and carried her like a football. Ellie started screaming to be put down.

Abra laid out on a blanket with Norah while Blaine took Ellie back in the water. Abra smelled a stench coming from Norah. She realized she forgot the diaper bag in the car. "Hey, Hon, I'm gonna run to the car and change Norah!" She hollered loud enough so Blaine could hear her over the crashing waves. Blaine waved wildly back.

Abra picked up Norah and headed to the car. When she came back out, Blaine was talking to a spectacular looking redhead that could have passed for a model. Abra looked again. This model was holding Abra's daughter. Abra tromped hard in the sand toward them. As she got closer she realized it was Jenna. Every time Abra had seen Jenna she had been wearing fairly loose clothing. She had never realized how perfect of a body Jenna had. She looked at her tiny hot pink bikini then looked down at her blue polka dotted one piece, disgusted. Also, was it her imagination or was Jenna flirting with her husband? Abra shook her head to get that ridiculous thought out of her mind. Blaine had always been an honest and faithful husband. She knew deep down she had nothing to worry about, but she still wasn't able to get rid of the horrible feeling in the pit of her stomach that something wasn't quite right with this picture. Abra thought she would be happy starting a career and having a family. She felt like she had it all. After last night, with Jenna reading to the girls and watching her play in the water with her husband and her daughter, Abra was feeling very uneasy with this new arrangement.

Blaine eventually looked over and noticed Abra standing there. Jenna was in the middle of talking, but cut herself off when she noticed she had lost Blaine's attention. They both headed towards Abra. "Look who I ran into," Blaine pointed out, as if Abra didn't know.

Abra smiled through gritted teeth. "Hi Jenna. Funny seeing you here. How are you?"

"I'm doing great. It's such a beautiful day, I just had to get some beach time." Abra set Norah down on the beach blanket they had sprawled out and let her roll around.

"Definitely the perfect day to be on the beach." Abra said.

"I don't want to disturb your family time. I just saw Blaine and Ellie and had to stop by and say hi. I'll see you guys later."

"Bye!" Blaine and Abra echoed. Abra watched Blaine's eyes carefully follow Jenna as she slowly walked away. Abra rolled her eyes, "You're a pig."

"What did I do?" Blaine said innocently.

"Whatever."

"You know you're the only one for me," Blaine said playfully tackling her and bringing her down on the blanket. Abra screamed, then laughed. Ellie and Norah jumped on top of them, wanting to join in the fun. Blaine sat up and pulled Norah onto his lap. Abra picked up Ellie. Blaine put his arm around Abra and they looked out across the ocean and watched the surfers in the distance catching the waves.

That evening, Abra was picking up the living room. It was always a little discouraging to Abra how she could spend so much time cleaning up after the girls and then within a matter of minutes, it would look like every toy the girls owned had been loaded into a confetti shooter and exploded all over the room. After she picked up the last toy and put it away, she fell back and collapsed on the sofa. Blaine came over shortly after and kissed her. He then made his best attempt at giving her sexy eyes.

"Why don't we see if my parents can keep the girls tonight?" He asked. Abra knew what Blaine was getting at, and she was not in the mood.

"Maybe another night. I'm so exhausted. Maybe another night, is that okay, Baby?"

"Yeah, I guess," he said shortly.

"Are you upset with me?" Abra asked.

"It's just, we haven't had any time to ourselves since we moved here. I thought that was going to be one of the plusses of moving near my family. They could babysit and we could start having date nights.

"I know, and we will. Just not tonight. Plus, it's not very fair to call them up at the last minute."

"Okay, fine" Blaine responded and walked out of the room.

The next day during lunch, Abra decided to eat in the teachers' lounge instead of sitting at her desk. When she walked in the lounge, she looked around for an empty table. She figured if she would sit by a table by herself, maybe someone would come over and sit by her. It gave her flashbacks of when she was in school on the first day in the cafeteria and not knowing anyone, not knowing where to sit or who to talk to. She overheard a couple of the teachers talking about how one of the other teachers' husband had been cheating on her.

"You know how it is. I mean, if you don't give it to him, men are like dogs. They'll just go find it somewhere else."

"That's just wrong, Amy."

Amy tilted her head to the side, "Am I wrong?"
As if Abra had just appeared out of thin air, Amy
looked at her, "You're new here, aren't you?"

"Yeah, I took over for Mrs. Gates class."

"Why don't you come over here and join us?"
They asked. Abra picked up her bag and diet soda and
went to sit with them. "Are you married?" Amy asked
while looking at her hand for a ring.

"Yeah, I am. His name is Blaine."

"Do you have any kids?" She asked.

"Yeah, I have two young daughters, Ellie and
Norah," Abra answered, cautiously.

"Well let me tell you, between work and kids,
you better make time for your hubby, or he'll just go
somewhere else.

"AMY!" the other lady yelled.

"What? Am I wrong?" Amy repeated.

"We don't even know her. Why would you say
something like that?"

Abra zoned out after that. She was reminded of
the night before and being too tired to spend time with
Blaine. She thought of Jenna and how easily it would
be for Blaine to have an affair and hide it. She tried to
tell herself that he was loyal and would never do

anything like that, but once that thought was incepted, there was no way of shaking it. She needed to make a change or she was going to lose Blaine.

"What do we have going on tonight?" Blaine asked that night.

Abra looked up, clueless. I don't think anything, why?"

Blaine brushed the hair off of her shoulder and kissed her neck. "I was hoping we would..." he trailed off.

"Oh," Abra leaned her head back. Did you want to call, or should I?" Abra smiled.

Blaine grabbed his phone. "Hey, Mom, Abra and I forgot we have something going on tonight." Abra stifled a giggle. "Would you be willing to watch the girls overnight?" There was a pause. "Thanks, we really appreciate it." He hung up.

"I feel a little guilty," Abra admitted. "Does this make us bad parents?"

"Absolutely," he said, kissing her again. "No, I don't think it makes us bad parents. I think it makes us a strong married couple."

After Pat picked up the girls, Blaine and Abra grabbed a beach blanket, two long stemmed wine glasses and a bottle of Hatteras Red, and went outside. He laid out the blanket, and they sat down. Blaine popped the cork on the wine, poured some in a glass, and handed it to Abra, then poured a glass for himself. He dug a small hole in the sand and set the bottle in it. He then picked up his glass and held it up in the air. "To us!" he said.

"To us!" Abra repeated, and they clanked their glasses together and took a sip. He took her glass from her and set both of the glasses next to them in the sand. He gently laid her down on the blanket. She pulled his shirt over his head, revealing a perfect six pack. She ran her hands over his biceps and scratched her nails down his back as he pulled her in close to him. He lifted her shirt up, exposing her flat tummy. He softly kissed down her body to her naval. He ran his hands softly up her thigh and up under her shorts. Blaine took off his pants and twirled them above his head. Abra hid behind her hands and giggled. Between the music, wine, the moonlight and the sound of the crashing waves, neither of them could imagine a more beautiful and romantic setting.

They woke up to something that could have been a painting in a museum. Laid out before them was the most beautiful sunrise; the oranges, pinks and purples melted into the horizon. The seagulls were squawking, and the waves gently crashing against the shore.

"How can you possibly have a bad day when you fall asleep like that and wake up to this?" He said, gesturing towards the ocean. Abra kissed him. "It was an incredible night."

They went back to the house, changed out of their clothes, then decided to go out for coffee before going to Blaine's parents to pick the girls up. Abra sipped on her caramel macchiato, while Blaine just got a plain black coffee. It had been a while since they had been able to go out for coffee together.

Ellie and Norah were running around in their pajamas when Blaine and Abra arrived at Blaine's parents' house. "I was just going to go get them dressed," Blaine's mom said.

"We'll just change them when we get home," Blaine said. They tried to pack them up, but they were having too much fun and didn't want to leave. Ellie fell to the ground and started screaming. Ellie followed suit. Finally, after a struggle, they were able to get them loaded in the Tahoe.

Chapter 10

During his next shift, Blaine was standing in the garage at the fire station talking to some of the other firefighters when he saw Jenna's car pull up. Confused that there might be something wrong with one of the girls, he rushed over to her. "Hey, I thought it might be nice to bring the girls to see where their daddy works," Jenna said. Blaine relaxed when he realized there was nothing wrong.

"What a nice surprise! I miss these girls like crazy when I'm not with them," he said, picking Ellie up and lifting her up above his head, making her laugh out loud.

"You caught me at just the right time. I was just about to get some lunch. Would you like to join me?" Jenna's face lit up.

"Absolutely! I would love to. Do you have someplace in mind?"

He thought a minute. "Actually, there is somewhere I would like to take you. Abra would kill me, but I have to show someone."

"Well then, let's go. Shall we?"

"After you."

Jenna was ecstatic. What was it he could possibly want to show her? They stopped at a nearby deli and continued on until they reached the pier. Blaine was beyond thrilled.

"I've never brought anyone here before. Abra thinks I'm crazy for wanting something so luxurious." Jenna walked around the yacht.

"This is incredible!" she commented. "Are we allowed in here?"

"I know the owner, and he said I could come here as long as he's not showing it to anyone, and we don't make a mess." They sat down and started eating.

"Are you going to buy it?"

"Hopefully, one day. Right now, I'm trying to save up some money. Well, that, and convince the wife to let me get it." Blaine responded, helping the girls with their lunch.

"You work hard. You deserve to splurge once in a while. I don't get it. If I was your wife, I'd let you buy it." She joked. He chuckled awkwardly.

"I should probably get back to work," he said, standing up and grabbing the wrappers from their deli sandwiches.

After lunch, Jenna brought the girls back home. She sat cross legged on the floor with Norah in her lap. Norah was playing with one of her toys. Jenna took it from her and hid it behind her back and Immediately Norah started screaming.

"Come on Norah, you know what you have to say. "Mama!" Norah cried.

"Good girl! Who am I?"

"Mama!" Norah cried again.

Jenna smiled, devilishly, "that's right, Baby Girl!" she said, and squeezed Norah tightly. It gave her such a wonderful feeling inside to hear Norah call her mom. She knew all she needed was a little motivation.

Jenna put the girls down for a nap and started snooping around the house. She rummaged through the drawers in their desk.

She walked past the bedroom and stopped. She opened up their nightstand and went through it. She couldn't help but smirk as an idea popped into her head. She fell back on the bed and rolled around. She picked up a picture sitting on top of the nightstand. It was a picture of Blaine and Abra on their wedding day. The frame had lightly painted seashells on it. No doubt one of Abra's creations that Blaine had been telling her about. Jenna rolled her eyes and tossed it on the bed beside her. She figured she had another fifteen minutes before the girls woke up. She laid there on his pillow. She put the pillow up to her face and inhaled deeply, breathing him in. He was such a creature of habit, she concluded. Still using the same hair gel he did in high school. She could smell it on him the day she came over for dinner that first night. That smell took her back to high school.

She jumped up off of the bed and pulled down her shorts. She took off her laced pink panties. She held them for a minute then tossed them under the bed. She then pulled her shorts back on and left the room to see if the girls were awake. They were still asleep, so she decided she wasn't going to stop snooping around yet.

She picked up Abra's laptop from the desk and opened it, watching as it came to life. She took her flash drive out of her pocket, plugged it in, and downloaded all of the pictures that were saved on the desktop. The rainbow pinwheel circled round and round. 80%, 83%... 90%...96%. Just then she heard the door open.

"I'm home!" Abra hollered out as she walked in.

The download was stuck on 99%. Finally, it said DOWNLOAD COMPLETE. She quickly yanked out the USB plug that she had in. "Hey! The girls are probably ready to wake from their nap," Jenna told Abra.

"Fantastic. I'll go check on them. I missed them like crazy today," Abra said, and disappeared into the other room. Jenna could hear Abra talking in the girls' bedroom. "There are my favorite girls!" she said excitedly, picking up Ellie and swinging her around the room. Once she set her down, Jenna handed Norah over. The three of them sat on the couch.

Ellie squirmed like Jell-O, but Abra just laughed. She laid Norah on a blanket on the floor, grabbed Ellie, and tossed her in the air. "I missed my favorite girls so much!" she said. Continuing to toss her making Ellie laugh hysterically. Jenna stood in the background, watching this display, her eyes throwing daggers at Abra. She finally excused herself and headed home.

The following morning Blaine woke up early. He finally had a day off work, and he was too anxious for it to begin. It had been a while since he was able to spend the whole day with his daughters. He walked down the hall to check on the girls. Both were sound asleep, so he went to the kitchen and started a pot of coffee. He went back to the bedroom to wait for the coffee to finish brewing. As he stepped in the doorway, two of the floorboards rubbed together, creating a loud, annoying creaking sound.

Abra sat straight up and whipped her head to face her clock. "Why didn't you wake me?" She gasped. "I'm supposed to be at school in twenty minutes!" She jumped out of bed, grabbed her black dress pants that were hanging up, and tried to pull them on as she ran to her closet to grab a top.

"I didn't think you had to be at school for another two hours?"

"We have a faculty meeting this morning so I have to be there early." Abra tripped over the pant leg and barely caught her balance on the side of the closet. "I didn't even finish my lesson plan for the day!" She grabbed a breakfast bar out of the cupboard, kissed Blaine and the girls, and ran out the door. She sat in the car and adjusted the rear view mirror. She took a look at herself and saw she had line marks all over her face from the pillow. "Ugh," she groaned and started poking and prodding at her face, trying to get the marks to disappear.

Blaine fed and dressed the girls. He was hoping to take the girls out on the beach that day. He opened the blinds to check the weather and was disappointed when he saw it was pouring rain out. He gathered some of the girls' toys and brought them out to the living room for them to play. Blaine walked over, grabbed the remote, and fell back onto the sofa while the girls played with a toy farm at his feet. Just as he sat down on the cushion, the doorbell rang. He looked up, surprised. They hadn't been expecting anyone. He peeked out the window and opened the door.

"Jenna, you're soaking wet. Come on in." Jenna shivered as she stepped inside.

"I'm sorry, did Abra forget to tell you I would be home today, and we wouldn't need you to watch the girls?"

"No, she told me. I ran out of gas down the road. I called someone to bring some, but I just didn't feel like sitting in the car while I waited."

"Of course. Come in. I was just gonna watch some TV."

"Thank you so much. I really appreciate it. It shouldn't be too long." Jenna came in and took off her coat.

"What a crummy day to run out of gas," Blaine pointed out as they sat down on the sofa.

"Just lucky, I guess," she said sarcastically.

Blaine flipped through the channels, but couldn't find anything worth watching.

"Maybe we could watch a movie?" Jenna said.

"Sure. The majority of our movies are animated. Hope that's okay."

Jenna walked over to their DVD tower to check out the selection. "How about *Despicable Me*?"

"Sure. If we don't finish it, you're more than welcome to borrow it." Blaine popped in the DVD and went back to the sofa. Jenna followed behind and sat closely beside him. Blaine slid down on the ground and played with Ellie and Norah, and it wasn't too long before Jenna scooted onto the floor and joined in.

Blaine looked down at his watch. An hour had passed. "Where is your friend coming from with gas?" He asked, suspiciously. He certainly didn't want Jenna to be sitting there with him when Abra came home.

Jenna checked the time. "It shouldn't be too much longer. I'll text him and see how much longer he'll be," she said, taking out her phone and quickly typing on the screen.

A couple of minutes later, she looked at her phone again. "Oh, it looks like it might be a while. He's in the middle of something. I told him I was safe and with a friend, so there was no hurry. I hope you don't mind.

"I can just take you to the gas station so we don't have to bother your friend."

"Oh no, it's no problem. He doesn't mind. This way we can finish the movie too."

Blaine sat back, feeling slightly uncomfortable. Once the movie ended, they realized it was nearly noon. "Were you planning on staying for lunch?" Blaine asked.

"It's okay. I don't want to impose any further than I already have."

"It's no imposition. It would be awkward if you sat and watched while the rest of us ate," he chuckled.

"If you insist," she said. Blaine went over to the fridge and started grabbing handfuls of lunch meat and cheeses and tossed them on the counter. Then he went and grabbed a container of chip dip and a bag of chips and placed them on the counter. "Help yourself to a sandwich or whatever else in the fridge." He made a sweeping motion with his hand toward the buffet on the counter. Jenna grabbed some bread, put some turkey and cheese on it, and squirted some mustard on. Blaine fed the girls, threw together a sandwich for himself, and carried the chips and dip to the sofa. "Don't tell Abra I was eating over here. She would have a cow," he said, joking.

"You're not allowed to eat where you want in your own house? It's like you're a prisoner."

Blaine looked at her quizzically, trying to determine if she was kidding or if she actually thought he was being held against his will.

"No, not at all. I can do whatever I want. I just know she doesn't like it when I eat over here, so I do what I can to not upset her."

Jenna shrugged. "Sounds like prison to me," she muttered under her breath.

Just then, the door opened. "Abra!" Blaine jumped up. The dip flew off his lap and splattered face down on the carpet. He rushed over to get some paper towels to clean up the mess. "You're home early," he pointed out.

"I didn't have time to pack a lunch, so I thought I'd come home for lunch today. She picked up the book off the counter and held it up to show. "What's going on here?"

"Jenna ran out of gas down the street. It was pouring out, so she came here to wait until someone brought gas for her.

"You couldn't drive her to a gas station?" Abra scorned.

"I asked, but she already talked to someone, and they're bringing gas."

"So the two of you have just been hanging out?" Blaine had no good answer, so he pretended not to hear her as he wiped up the carpet.

"Uh, I think I'll go wait in my car. My friend just texted me and said he'd be there in a minute."

"Bye," Abra waved, trying to be friendly.

"I'm sorry. I shouldn't have come here."

Abra let out a deep sigh. "No, it's fine. Sorry about you running out of gas. You sure you don't want a ride to your car?"

"No thanks. It's not that far, and the rain slowed down."

"Okay, see you tomorrow," Abra closed the door behind her.

Jenna smiled the whole way to her car. She hopped in behind the steering wheel, turned the ignition, and sped away.

Chapter 11

It had been a week since Abra had sent the e-mail to Sadie with no response. Every day Abra would get up and the first thing she would do was check her e-mail to see if Sadie had written. She was trying to put toys away while Ellie and Norah trailed behind her, pulling everything she just put away back out. All of a sudden, the doorbell rang. Abra jogged through the house to the front door. When she opened the door, she saw herself: her eyes, her nose. If Abra were to be stretched out, you would get Sadie. She had a long, skinny body and long straight hair, as opposed to Abra with her tightly curled hair and short stature. When they stood by each other, there was no question they were sisters.

"Sadie!" Abra screeched, grabbing the woman and holding her tight.

"Hey Sis!"

"Come in, come in!" Abra pulled her in the house. "I can't believe you're actually here!" Abra grabbed Sadie again and didn't want to let go.

"It's so good to see you. When I read the e-mail, I couldn't get here soon enough," Sadie exclaimed. "I'm so sorry for not getting in touch with you sooner. I tried to call you on your wedding day, but..." Sadie trailed off.

"I know. It's okay," Abra responded.

"I didn't think you wanted anything to do with me. Not that I would blame you. I knew dad was wrong. I was just too chicken to stand up to him."

Abra nodded, "That's all in the past. I think it's time for a new beginning."

Sadie let out a sigh of relief. "I couldn't agree more."

Ellie and Norah were running around. Abra grabbed Ellie as she tried to run past her. "Ellie, Norah, this is your Auntie Sadie." Ellie waved. Norah blew bubbles in response. "Let's go play in the living room while your Aunt Sadie and I catch up," Abra said, guiding them through the halls.

"I feel like you're a completely different person now. Look at you. You have your own home. You're a wife and a mother."

"And a teacher," Abra added.

"How wonderful! I always knew you would make an excellent teacher."

Abra smiled. "How about you? I'm sure you have a million different stories from all of the adventures you've been on."

"Oh, you have no idea! I dated this guy for a couple months after you left. He was smart, rich, funny and over-the-top dreamy," Sadie explained.

"Sounds like he had it all," Abra commented.

"Yes, he did. Including a wife and two kids."

Abra's mouth dropped, and she burst out laughing. "You sure know how to pick 'em," she replied, shaking her head.

"I know. I'm a magnet for them. So, after we broke up, I decided to become a flight attendant."

"That sounds like the perfect job for you. You've always loved traveling."

"Yeah, too bad I never get to leave the airport to enjoy wherever we are."

"I guess there are down sides to any job." As Abra said this, she thought about how she hated the time she spent away from home when she was at work.

Abra and Sadie walked into the kitchen. "Jenna made fresh banana bread if you want some."

"That sounds delicious. Who's Jenna?"

"Oh, sorry, she's the nanny,"

"Ahhh," Sadie said sticking her nose up playfully. Thought you got away from that? Miss. Moneybags needs hired help?"

Abra rolled her eyes. "It's not like that. Blaine and I are both working. Someone has to watch the girls. It's not like how we grew up. Jenna doesn't live with us. She just watches the girls during the day. We looked into daycares, but they were too expensive. Plus I watched that TV special on the kids being neglected and abused in daycares. You have to be so careful. Jenna's fantastic. You'll have to meet her." As they sat around and caught up on one another's lives, Abra asked the question she had been dreading. "How are Mom and Dad?"

Sadie looked away, her eyes starting to tear up. "Dad's sick, Abra."

"What do you mean?"

"He's been sick for a while now."

"Sadie, what does he have?"

"He has stage 4 lung cancer."

"What does that mean?"

"Well, there's not a stage 5," she snapped back.

"Oh Sadie, I'm so sorry. I had no idea." Abra immediately felt guilty for not being a part of her family.

"After I got your e-mail, I knew it was a sign that I was supposed to reconnect with you." Sadie had always been the type to believe in horoscopes, tarot cards, and signs. Abra hated to be the one to tell her that you can find signs anywhere if you look hard enough. For example, the people that rearrange, add, and subtract numbers to get the answer they're looking for. Or you can be looking too hard and miss the obvious, like the man who was waiting to be saved by God and passed up the boat and helicopter God sent to save him. Abra decided it wasn't the time to give her a reality check. Sadie's outlook on life was something that Abra absolutely adored about her. She was glad to see that she had not changed over the past couple of years.

As they nibbled on their banana bread, Sadie got real quiet. "I have a confession," she finally said. "I didn't just come here to catch up." There was a long pause. "I came to bring you home."

Abra nearly choked on her bread. "What? Are you kidding? Dad would take one look at me and fall over from a heart attack."

Sadie turned defensive. "Look, this thing between you and dad has been going on for way too long. This might be the only chance you have to make up with him. I know you, and if something happened, you would never be able to forgive yourself." Sadie leaned back in the chair and folded her arms. "I'm not leaving unless you come with me."

Abra let out a huge sigh. "Look, I'm working now. I can't just up and leave."

Sadie shot her a look and scooted deeper into her chair, affirming that she meant what she said. "It's only Thursday. We can catch a flight tomorrow."

"That's way too soon," Abra interjected.

"Time is of the essence right now, Abra,"

"Okay, I'll talk to Blaine and see what I can do."

"Thank you, thank you!" Sadie grabbed Abra in a tight embrace. For the life of her, Abra could not figure out why this was so important to Sadie. If she didn't make up with her father, she was the one who would have to live with the guilt. Why was Sadie the one who had to apologize in the first place? She wasn't the one who did anything wrong. Then again, that was typical Sadie, trying to patch up the family. Unfortunately, her family seemed to be beyond patchwork.

Later that night, Blaine and Abra were playing gin rummy.

"So, I had a visitor today."

"Oh?"

"Yeah...it was Sadie."

Blaine looked over his cards and raised his eyebrows. "What did she want?" Abra hadn't told Blaine she had e-mailed Sadie a few weeks prior. "I mean, what brought her here?" He rephrased. He wasn't sure if this was good news or not. He knew how close the two sisters had been when they were growing up, but he was also there for the fall out. He was the reason behind their rift, after all. Blaine always felt responsible for Abra not communicating with her family.

"Blaine...my father...he has cancer. They don't know how long he has."

"Oh Sweetie, I'm so sorry." He took her in his arms, not sure what else to do or say. "Are you ok?" He asked. Abra shrugged. He looked her square in the eyes. "What do you want?"

"I want to not deal with it. I want my dad to be okay and for him to start talking to me and for things to go back to the way they were. I want my daughters to know their grandparents and aunt."

Blaine forced a smile. "Well, I don't think that's in the cards." He smiled, putting a card back on the deck.

Abra winced at his horrible joke and lined her cards up by suit and numerical order.

"Maybe I should go. I would hate for something to happen to him and me not try to make things right. I could never forgive myself for that."

"I think you should. Not for him, but for yourself. Your dad has had this hold on you your whole life. This might be the closure you need to be set free."

Abra realized that Blaine was right. Her father had a hold on her so tight that, even 600 miles away, she felt like she was wearing a corset. She felt like one of those stress relief toys that you squeeze and her eyes bulge out. "I'll check with Jenna to see if she can be available in case you need any help with the girls while I'm gone." She flipped her cards on the deck upside-

down and laid out her hand. "There's something else."
Abra paused. "Sadie flew in this morning. I kinda told
her she could crash here tonight."

"What? Where is she?"

"She went to visit some friends who live down
here. She'll be back in a couple of hours. I hope you're
not mad," she said.

"No, of course not. I think it's wonderful you
two are made up and are getting along again. How long
is she staying here?"

"She has to be back at work on Monday, so
she'll be here until Sunday afternoon, I guess...
unless...."

"Unless what?"

"Sadie had mentioned me going home with her
for the weekend, you know, to try to talk to my dad.
She would have to stay here tonight though." Abra
waited for Blaine to blow up. She hadn't even thought
twice about having Sadie stay. She knew she should
have checked with Blaine before she invited house
guests, but when Sadie asked if she could stay, Abra
responded reflexively.

"Well, I guess we better make sure the guest room is set up for her," he said, smiling. Abra wrapped her arms around him, relieved.

Jenna walked in that next morning and saw a tall, beautiful woman with black hair. Jenna looked at her with hatred and distrust. Not only was she gorgeous, she was with her girls. This mysterious woman was infringing on her territory. She was holding Norah. "Hi! You must be Jenna! I'm Abra's sister, Sadie. It's so nice to meet you!" She pumped Jenna's hand enthusiastically. Jenna scanned her up and down. She was wearing a cloth headband that pulled her shiny black hair out of her face, a tank top that came midway down her thighs, and jeans that had patches and designs covering them.

"Nice to meet you too," Jenna choked out. "Where's Abra?"

"She ran to the store to pick up some things for her trip, so I said I'd watch the girls so she could run out real quick this morning. I've missed so much time with my nieces because of my job. It's hard to get off work."

Jenna remembered what Abra had said about her sister and the fallout between them. She had never even met Ellie and Norah before, and now she just drops in out of nowhere, and Abra leaves them with her. Jenna had half a mind to report Abra to children's services. She clearly was an unfit mother.

"Where is she going?" Jenna asked urgently.

"Our father is very sick, so I came to bring Abra home to spend time with the family. We're not exactly sure how much longer he has." Sadie began to tear up.

Abra soon came in weighed down with shopping bags. Jenna rushed over to help her. "I see you two have met," she said to Jenna.

"Abra, what can I make for dinner tonight?" Jenna offered, desperately trying to reclaim her territory.

"Actually, in celebration of being reunited with Sadie, and the fact that I'm going out of town, I thought we could go out. I was thinking, we should go to Tale of the Whale." A spark flickered in Jenna's eye. There was no reason for her to stick around. "You can join us if you want. You're like part of the family now."

It should be my family, Jenna thought to herself, but bit her tongue. "I wouldn't want to impose, but I have to admit, that is one of my favorite restaurants," Jenna said.

Later that evening when Abra got home from work, Blaine threw Abra's suitcase in the back of their Tahoe, and they headed to the restaurant. Jenna made sure she sat beside Blaine. When Blaine made a joke, Jenna would laugh hysterically. Abra stood up and excused herself to go to the restroom. Blaine started talking about some of the awful calls he's had to respond to. His hand was resting on the table. Jenna lightly laid her hand on top of his. Sadie raised an eyebrow. She did not like the scene that was unfolding before her. The way Jenna twirled her red hair around her finger, the way she batted her long eyelashes and nodded her head at everything her sister's husband said, made her very uneasy.

"That must be so hard on you. The things you have to hear and deal with day after day."

"It can be. Luckily I have an amazing wife I can sound off to at the end of the day," he said, and took his hand out from under Jenna's. Sadie smiled, 'Good for you, Blaine,' she wanted to say out loud, but refrained.

As soon as Jenna saw Abra walking back to the table, she sat straight up and smiled a brilliant smile at her. Sadie looked first to Abra, her lovely, yet naïve, sister. Abra smiled back, oblivious. Sadie then looked to Blaine, who looked slightly uncomfortable.

"What did I miss?" Abra asked.

"Blaine was just telling this hilarious story," Jenna responded.

Blaine jumped in. "I was telling them about the time when I closed the bedroom door and you woke up in the middle of the night not realizing it and crashed right into it."

"Ha...ha" Abra said, taking it lightly. "There are a few stories about you I would like to share with the group since you're being so generous."

"Uh oh," Blaine put his hands up, surrendering. He leaned over and kissed Abra. Sadie watched the couple in adoration. She hoped she could find someone who treated her as well as Blaine treated Abra.

Chapter 12

After dinner, Blaine dropped Abra and Sadie off at the airport and returned home. He didn't know what he would do for the next couple of days without his better half. He read the girls a bedtime story, put them to bed, and then went to sit on the back deck. He sat, listening to the waves crashing against the shore. He was starting to doze off himself, when all of a sudden he heard the door open in the house. He stood up and rushed inside.

"Hey Blaine!"

"Jenna? What are you doing here?"

"I have a huge favor to ask of you. My house is being fumigated tomorrow. Would it be too much to ask if I could stay here tonight?"

"I guess so. As much as you've helped us out, it's the least I can do." he said hesitantly.

"Thank you so much! I really appreciate it. If there's ever anything I can do to pay you back, just say the word," she said, placing her hand on his shoulder.

"I have no problem with you staying here, but you could have just called or texted. You didn't need to make a special trip out," Blaine pointed out.

"Oh, it's not a big deal. I had to go right past your house to get home anyway, so I thought I would stop by and check. Plus I thought you might be lonely with Abra gone. I can stick around for a little while if you want."

"No, I think I'm just gonna watch some TV and go to bed. Thanks though."

"Ok well, thanks again for letting me stay. You're a lifesaver."

"Not a problem at all. I should probably go check on the girls. I'll see you later."

"I'll let myself out," Jenna called after him.

Blaine was down the hall, and Jenna was about to walk out the door, when she saw Blaine's phone light up on the counter. She looked around, then looked down at the phone. She smiled an evil smile and picked it up.

When Abra and Sadie landed in Ohio, Abra called to let Blaine know they made it safely. She almost couldn't speak when the voice that answered on the other end was not Blaine's, but a peppy woman's voice. It was Jenna. She told Abra about her house and how Blaine had allowed her to stay the night.

"Your husband is so amazing! I don't know what I would have done without him."

Immediately, Abra asked to talk to Blaine.

"He went to check on the girls. I can have him call you later?" Jenna offered.

"Yes, please do!" Abra said through gritted teeth and hung up. "Stay away from my husband!" She yelled at the phone. She looked up to see Sadie staring at her, looking startled. "Sorry," she said quickly.

"What was that all about?" Sadie asked.

Abra took a deep breath and explained that Jenna would be staying the night.

"What? While you're out of town? Hmm...I'd keep my eyes on that one, Abra."

"I trust my husband. I know he would never do anything to hurt me, and he would never cheat on me."

"I realize that, but from your reaction, it doesn't sound like you trust Jenna. Why don't you hire someone else to watch the girls? I mean, come on. I find it a little odd that the day you leave, she decides to move in."

"She can try all she wants. She's not gonna get my man." Abra joked. Sadie smiled awkwardly. "Come on, Blaine ain't gonna give up all this," Abra said striking a pose. They both burst out laughing. Abra tried to put on a front pretending it really didn't bother her, but inside she was ready to scream. It didn't take long for Abra and Sadie to feel like sisters again.

It had been a couple of hours since Jenna informed Abra she would be staying at her house and Abra was ready to explode. So when her phone rang and Blaine's photo popped up on the screen, Abra couldn't answer fast enough. "Exactly what were you thinking, telling Jenna she could stay there without even consulting me?" It came out a lot harsher than Abra had anticipated, but it had been building up inside of her.

"I was thinking she's been there for us when we needed her, and this time she needed our help. I didn't think it was a big deal. Plus, she would be driving back here early the next morning to watch our daughters anyways, so it just made sense. I'm sorry I didn't consult you, but I didn't think you would have a big problem with it."

"You didn't think I would have a problem with you having a sleepover with another woman while I was away?"

"You're right. I wasn't thinking. I'm really sorry. Please forgive me?" Even through the phone, Abra could picture Blaine making his adorable puppy dog look that he always made when she was upset with him. She could never stay mad at him when he gave her that look.

"I just wish you would have said something first. I don't really like the way she talks to you. It seems very flirty to me," Abra said, analyzing and recollecting the past couple hours in her mind.

"Ab, Sweetie, don't even put those thoughts in your head." She's our daughters' nanny. Nothing has or is going on between us. You should know that. She can flirt all she wants."

"Still," Abra interjected, "the fact that she has no problem flirting with you in front of your wife. It's just...disrespectful. She must not think much of me if she's willing to do that."

"Yeah, don't let it get to you though. You can trust me. I hope you know that." Blaine paused for a moment.

"Did you want to find someone new to watch the girls? You remember how difficult it was finding Jenna. You don't want to go through that again."

"Yeah, I guess you're right. Maybe I'm just being a little paranoid."

"You know I love you. You're the only one for me, and nothing will ever change that." Abra gushed at Blaine's words.

"I love you too." Abra replied.

"Are we okay?" Blaine asked.

"We're good. I'll call you in the morning. Love you, Baby." Abra felt a lot better after she talked to Blaine.

As she and Sadie fought their way through the airport and got a rental car, Abra realized how close she was to having to face her father. Her heart started to race and she had what felt like a million hyperactive butterflies taking over her stomach. She took a deep breath, trying to control her nerves.

Abra felt like a teenager as she and Sadie stepped inside their childhood home. Sadie called out to their mom as she walked in the door. "Sadie, is that you?" Abra heard the familiar voice. It brought tears to her eyes. A lump stuck in her throat, and butterflies continued to take over her stomach. Abra started to back out the door.

"Sadie, I don't think I can do this." She whispered.

Sadie grabbed her hand. "Don't you dare run away now!" Even though Sadie was older, for the first time, Abra felt like the younger sister. "This has gone on way too long, and it stops now! I don't want you to regret this one day."

"Sadie?" The voice called out louder. "Yeah, Mom, it's me!" Sadie yelled back.

A fragile, thin lady walked into the living room. "I brought someone with me," Sadie warned Leah.

Leah squinted to get a better look. "Abra, is that you?"

"Yeah, Mama, it's me."

Leah made her way as fast as she could to her estranged daughter. She stopped in front of her and raised her hand to touch her daughter's cheek.

"How's Dad?" Abra asked.

Her mom closed her eyes and shook her head. "Not good, sweetheart. The Doctors say he doesn't have much longer." She looked down. "How's...your husband."

"He's doing good." Abra lifted one side of her mouth in a half smile. "You have two granddaughters." Leah started sobbing. "Can I see him?" Abra asked, going back to her father.

"Oh Abra, I don't know. He's already so sick. I'm afraid the stress from seeing you might be too much for him right now."

Sadie stepped forward and put a hand in front of Abra, pushing her back. "Mom, that's ridiculous and you know it! Dad is dying! She deserves to make amends with him."

"Abra...I love you. You know that. It almost killed your father when you walked out...."

"You mean got thrown out," Sadie yelled.

Leah held up her hand. "He had finally healed, and now you've come back to tear open the scars."

"Mom, that's not it at all. It killed me just as much to leave. This is my final chance to make things right with him....and you." Leah shut her eyes, took a deep breath and stepped aside, allowing Abra to walk passed her. "Thank you," Abra said, wiping a tear from her eye. She paused and looked at Sadie. "You coming?"

"No, I think this is something you have to do on your own." Abra realized she was right and continued down the hall.

As she walked through the halls that used to be so familiar to her, she felt like a complete stranger. She remembered running through those very same halls. The house had seemed gigantic to her. She looked around. There was no indication that she had even lived here. She saw pictures of Sadie hanging on the wall, but none of her. She got to her parents' room and stopped outside. She had been praying for the day she would get to see her family again for years, but she never thought it would actually happen. Now that it was, she was completely unprepared. She slowly peeked in, easing herself inside as if she were testing the temperature of water before diving in. "Dad?" She didn't recognize her own voice. It sounded so tiny and mouse-like.

"Sadie?" He asked.

"No, Dad, it's me...Abra." She looked in at the man lying in the bed. This was not the man she knew. The man who had always had a young, boyish face. The man Abra had always thought was invincible was now so delicate and fragile. His voice came out rough and raspy. He looked at her hard and long. Abra had silently prepared herself for the worst as she waited for his response. She had to at least try talking to him, or, like Sadie said, she would regret it the rest of her life.

"Abra? The name sounds familiar. I think I used to have a daughter by that name."

Abra wept audibly. This was a lot harder than she thought. Not speaking was a lot easier than being disowned to your face. "Daddy, please," she cried. He turned his head, but Abra could tell he was crying too. "You know I never meant to hurt you or mom. I had to follow my heart. Blaine is a great guy and we have a wonderful life together." She paused. "But I'm not here to talk about Blaine. I just wanted you to know that I love you. After all we've been through and everything that's happened, I still love you."

At this point, he was sobbing, which caused him to have a coughing fit. Abra rushed to the bed. Leah came rushing in to see what was going on. She had apparently been listening from the hallway. "Dad? Are you okay?" He gasped for air between coughs, but still managed to nod.

"See! What did I tell you? He was doing great today then you came here and upset him!"

Leah hastily made her way to the bed and leaned in. "Are you okay, Aaron? Can I get you something?" She turned to Abra. "I think it's best if you leave," she said coldly. Aaron said something, but they couldn't understand it. "What did you say, Dear?"

"She can stay. I have something to say to her."

"Aaron, are you sure?" He nodded. Leah got a concerned look and walked away. Abra was shaking. She had no idea what he was about to say. He motioned for her to sit on the bed beside him. She slowly made her way to the bed and sat down.

"As a parent, you try to do what is best for your kids. You feel like you know best, but sometimes, parents make mistakes too." He tried to lift the corner of his mouth up into a smile, but it was weak. "I've had a lot of time to think about things in my life, and you kept creeping into my mind. One of my biggest regrets was letting you walk out of my life." Abra smiled through her tears. "I can't change the past, but I want you to know how truly sorry I am for everything I've put you through."

Abra wrapped her arms around her father. It felt so foreign and wonderful. "I thought you would like to know...you have two granddaughters. Would you like to see their pictures?"

"I would like that very much." Abra took out her cell phone and went through all of the pics until she found some of Ellie and Norah.

"They're beautiful. They look just like you."

"Thank you." When he finished looking at the pictures, he handed back the phone and laid back on the bed. "I'm feeling really tired right now. I think I'll rest for a bit." She leaned in and hugged him and kissed him on the head the way he used to do to her when she was a young girl.

Abra walked out of the room and closed the door behind her. Sadie had been standing outside the door, waiting for her. Sadie lightly grabbed Abra by the arm. "How did everything go?" she asked, concerned.

Abra looked at Sadie for a moment, then smiled. "It went as well as it could have possibly gone, considering the circumstances."

Sadie took Abra's hand and squeezed it gently. "I knew that it would," Sadie said, and they headed into the other room to find their mom.

Leah was in the kitchen making tea, trying to calm herself down. She offered some to Abra and Sadie. They brought their tea over to the table and sat down.

"How've you been through all of this, Ma?" Abra asked.

"It's been hard sitting here, helpless while you watch the man you love waste away. I'm sorry I snapped earlier. It's been unbearable. I try to protect him, but I don't know how. You have no idea how happy I am that the two of you made up. I wish it could have been under different circumstances."

The three of them stayed up until one in the morning catching up on one another's lives.

Chapter 13

When Blaine got home from being on call that night, the house was quiet. Too quiet, he thought. That was never a good sign with two little girls running around the house. He looked out the back door and saw Jenna sitting at the picnic table on the back deck. There was a red tablecloth over the picnic table with two long-stemmed candles lit in the center. Jenna had set two dinner plates out on the picnic table. She had his favorite meal all spread out.

"Uh, Jenna, what's going on here?" he asked.

"I just thought it would be nice to eat outside tonight. I fed the girls, and they've already been bathed and put to bed." She glanced down at the baby monitor sitting by her plate.

Blaine looked at her, confused. There was nothing wrong with having dinner with her. He didn't feel like eating alone. Jenna had been a huge help with the girls with Abra being gone, and it was so nice of her to go through all of the trouble. She had obviously spent a lot of time on dinner. He didn't want to offend her by not eating. Sure, the candles threw him for a loop, but he was starving, and his favorite meal was in front of him, so he sat down. Blaine felt a little uncomfortable having a candlelit dinner with someone that was not his wife so after a few minutes he stood up. "This was very thoughtful of you, Jenna, but it's been a really long day. So if it's okay with you, I'm just going to finish eating inside. I wanna check on my daughters and head to bed." He picked up his plate and started to head inside. As he grabbed the doorknob he turned around. "I don't know if maybe I'm reading this wrong or not, but Jenna, you are considered my employee. I hope you know I love my wife, and this was nothing more than a friendly dinner."

Jenna tried to look shocked and embarrassed. "You thought I did this to seduce you? Blaine, I just wanted to thank you for letting me stay over. I figured it was such a beautiful night, so I wanted to eat outside."

"What about the candles?"

"In case you haven't noticed, it's dark out. I just thought it might be nice. I'm so sorry if I gave you the wrong impression," she said, trying to avoid his eyes.

Blaine turned bright red. Now it was his turn to be embarrassed. "Jenna, I'm truly sorry. I just wanted to make sure we both knew the boundaries around here. Obviously, I was horribly wrong. Now that I am completely humiliated, I think I should probably eat inside. Thank you for all the trouble you went through making all of this." He gestured towards the table and then slipping inside.

Jenna blew out the candles and carried everything back into the house. "Okay, Blaine, apparently you still need a little more convincing. Maybe I need to step it up a little bit. After all, desperate times called for desperate measures," Jenna said to herself and left the house.

The next morning, Blaine asked Jenna if she would mind watching the girls that evening. She quickly agreed. Charlie had invited him and some of his guy friends over for a poker night. With Blaine being new to the area and not knowing a whole lot of people, he thought it would be a good idea to go and make some new guy friends. They needed one more guy, so Blaine had asked Sam if he wanted to play. Sam told Blaine he would pick him up on the way, being that he drove past his house on the way to Charlie's.

Blaine was still getting ready when Sam showed up on the doorstep and rang the doorbell. "Can you grab that, Jenna?" I'll be right down!"

"Sure, no problem," Jenna hollered back. She quickly made her way over to the door, carrying Norah on her hip. When she opened the door she was greeted by a man in khaki shorts and a dark blue polo shirt. He flashed her an award-winning smile.

"You must be Jenna," he said, extending his hand. Jenna smiled and let him inside.

"You must be Sam. Blaine's still getting ready. He'll be down in a minute. Did you want anything to drink?" She asked, trying to be a good host. He shook his head, clearly hypnotized by Jenna's beauty.

As Jenna lightly danced around the house, getting herself a drink, she realized she could really get used to this life--the life where this was her home and she wasn't just a guest. The life where she was Mrs. Blaine Ryan. Jenna turned around and realized Sam was standing directly behind her. He was so close that she almost ran into him.

"I've heard a lot about you from Blaine." Jenna's powdered skin turned a deep pink, making her freckles stand out. Maybe her plan was working after all. She beamed. She at least had him talking about her, and from Sam's tone when he said that, they weren't bad things. Her high was short-lived, and her smile faded once he continued. "But he never said how beautiful you were." Jenna forced a smile and stomped into the other room.

Jenna couldn't take her eyes off of Blaine as he walked down the steps. He looked exceptionally good in his shorts and tight T-Shirt. "Thanks for watching the girls, Jenna. I shouldn't be too late."

"No problem. See you soon," she said as he walked out the door. She smiled to herself inside. Abra was out of town. When was she ever going to have this opportunity again. She knew exactly what she needed to do.

"So tell me more about this Jenna. Is she dating anyone?" Sam asked Blaine on the drive to Charlie's.

Blaine couldn't care less about his nanny's personal life. He shrugged his shoulders, "I don't think so," Blaine said.

"Will you give me her number?" Sam asked anxiously.

"No, Sam, I don't want you dating my nanny."

"Aw, come on, man," Sam begged as they walked up the driveway leading to Charlie's house.

"Absolutely not. She is off limits."

"How come?" Sam asked.

"You know perfectly well why not," Blaine said just as Charlie opened the door.

As they sat around the poker table, Sam still wouldn't stop talking about Jenna. "I can't believe Abra let you hire such a hot nanny!" he said.

Blaine rolled his eyes behind his cards. "First of all, Abra doesn't 'let me' do anything."

"Way to save your dignity," his brother said, laughing.

Blaine ignored him. "Second, it doesn't matter how hot she is." He held up his hand, flashing his wedding ring. "I know this may not be something some of you understand," he looked at Sam, who slept with a different girl every week, and shot a quick glance at Charlie, who'd had an affair. "But this," he pointed at his ring, "means something to me."

Charlie looked down, embarrassed. Sam was proud of his reputation and turned to fist- bump Charlie. Charlie shook his head, "No, no," he said quickly.

"Dude, you gotta hook me up with that sweet nanny of yours!" Sam kept nagging.

"Forget it, Sam. She's a great nanny. It was hard enough finding her. I don't want to go through that again after you dump her the next day."

"Oh yeah!" Sam said, proud, trying to fist-bump Blaine. Blaine shook his head, rolled his eyes, and looked back at his cards. The whole time, Charlie was really quiet.

All of a sudden, he stood up and announced he was going to the kitchen to get more beer. Blaine noticed something was up, so he followed him in to the kitchen.

"You okay?" Blaine asked.

"Why did you have to go and flaunt my mistakes in front of everyone? You know, you were the only one I told about the affair. I thought I could trust you."

"You *can* trust me. What are you talking about? I didn't say anything,"

"Then what was that look supposed to mean?" Charlie asked.

"Sorry, man, I'm sure no one else knew why I was looking at you. It was just a look. I was just getting really annoyed with Sam not leaving me alone about setting him up with Jenna."

"I don't think you realize how guilty I feel about what I did, and then having you rub my nose in how perfect you are, and how I screwed everything up, doesn't help." Charlie was trying to talk quietly so no one else could hear.

"I am by no means perfect, and I never claimed to be. I'm sorry if that's what you thought I was insinuating." Charlie grabbed the beer from the fridge, slammed the door and started to walk out. Blaine grabbed his arm. "Charlie, I'm sorry. I didn't mean anything by it. Honest." Charlie started to calm down.

"Please, just don't say anything else. I don't want anyone else to know." Blaine nodded, "I won't," and they joined the table again.

When Blaine got home late that night, he was feeling slightly tipsy from all the beer he drank at the poker game. Usually he didn't drink that much, but it had been so long since he'd been able to have a guy's night with Charlie and his friends, and he was having a great time.

Jenna was sitting in the hot tub holding a glass of wine. The bottle and another glass were sitting on the picnic table. "Welcome home!" she greeted Blaine, jumping up to get out of the hot tub. "I hope you don't mind. This hot tub is so relaxing. I could just lie back in here all day."

Blaine raised an eyebrow at her. "Um, I guess that's ok. Where are the girls?" Blaine asked urgently.

"They're fast asleep," Jenna said, gesturing towards the baby monitor sitting on the picnic table.

"I would prefer that you stay in the house when you're babysitting. If something happened and the girls needed you, you wouldn't be able to get to them in time. So I don't mind you using the hot tub, but not while you're in charge of the girls.

"I figured it was ok, being that I brought the baby monitor out. I'm sorry. I won't do it again," Jenna said, carefully stepping out of the hot tub. Water was dripping off of her bathing suit onto the deck as she tiptoed over to the bottle of wine and poured Blaine a glass.

"Oh, I shouldn't drink. I've already had enough, and Abra would kill me if she found out." Blaine looked around and saw Jenna's long, oversized t-shirt sitting on the picnic table. He grabbed it. "Here, maybe you should put this on," he said, trying not to look directly at her. Jenna raised an eyebrow, grabbed the t-shirt, and forcefully pulled it on over her head.

"So why would Abra be upset about you drinking? It's not like you drove home."

"I know, but she would still over-exaggerate the situation. I had a little drinking problem in college, and she's afraid I'll step back to my old ways.

Jenna laughed. "Who didn't have a drinking problem in college?"

"Yeah, mine was pretty bad though."

"Oh really? What happened?"

"Shortly after we started going out, I went to a frat party. She had an exam the following day, so she didn't go. Anyway, I got completely trashed and ended up waking up in a strange dorm room on the opposite side of campus with no recollection of how I got there."

Jenna's mouth dropped and she let out a laugh. "Wow, I can see why Abra might have been a little less than pleased about that."

"Less than pleased?" He raised the sleeve of his left arm to reveal a scar the shape of a crescent moon.

"This is from where she threw my football trophy at me."

Jenna's eyes got huge. She remembered when Blaine had received the trophy, senior year. "Oh my God! I would never have pegged Abra for the violent type." Jenna took her perfectly polished finger and touched the scar. She touched it so lightly that it felt like a feather tickling Blaine's skin. He shivered beneath her touch. For a second they looked in each others eyes. Jenna's heart skipped a beat. They were having a moment. The night couldn't have been going better.

Just as quickly as that moment came, it passed. Screaming came echoing through the monitor into their ears. It was Ellie. Blaine started to stand up but Jenna stopped him. "I'll grab her, don't worry. I'll be right back." Jenna stood up and went inside, leaving the monitor sitting on the table. She picked up Ellie and sat in the rocker. She gently rocked Ellie and started singing the beautiful lullaby her mom had sung to her. Jenna had always been told she had an excellent voice. It didn't take long, and Ellie was out cold again. Jenna placed her back in her crib and went back out to the man of her dreams.

"That was really beautiful," Blaine commented as she walked out on the deck.

Jenna covered her mouth, "Oh no, you heard me!" She pretended to be embarrassed. Blaine smiled and looked down at the monitor. "I forgot that was out here. I'm mortified," she said, lowering her head.

"Don't be. You have a marvelous singing voice," he said.

"Thank you. I've never sung in front of anyone before." Just then she looked down and noticed he had helped himself to a glass of wine. "Changed your mind, I see," she pointed at the glass.

"Yeah, what the heck. What Abra doesn't know won't hurt her."

"It'll be our little secret," she said, taking a sip of her wine. Just as she started to set her glass back on the table, the glass caught on the edge of the table and toppled over. The blood red wine exploded all over Jenna's white shirt. The glass smashed against the floor. Jenna yelled a chain of vulgar words as she jumped up, then quickly apologized for her language.

Blaine laughed it off, "I'll grab a rag," he said, running back inside the house.

Jenna quickly ran to the table and grabbed her shorts and pulled out a pill bottle. She opened it up, dropped one of them in Blaine's glass, swished it around, and put it back in its place. Blaine came back out with a wet rag. He walked over and started to reach toward her to blot off the stain. He fumbled with the rag for a minute.

"Um...hmm...maybe you should..." He handed Jenna the rag. Jenna rolled her eyes and started working on the stain. Blaine got down on his hands and knees and started cleaning up the broken shards.

"I'm so sorry. I can't believe I broke your beautiful glass. I'm such a klutz!" Jenna said.

"Don't worry about it. You didn't get cut or anything, did you?" Jenna shook her head. Blaine went back inside to throw away the glass pieces. "I guess that's what I get for going against my wife. I told you I wasn't supposed to drink," he joked.

A spark shot from Jenna's eyes, but Blaine missed it. "Don't be ridiculous. One glass isn't gonna hurt you," she persuaded.

"Nah, I think the moment has passed," he responded.

Jenna pouted and picked up his glass to bring it over to him and wave it under his nose. "Aw, come on. I can't be the only one drinking."

"Fine, but you can't tell Abra. If she finds out I was drinking at the poker game, and then drank more when I got home, she'll have a fit."

"Your secret's safe with me" she said softly. Jenna paused and watched him take a long drink. Waiting. He finished the glass in just a few gulps. He exhaled loudly when he was finished. "See, no harm done," Jenna confirmed.

She grabbed the bottle off the table. "Ready for a refill?" she asked eagerly.

Blaine chuckled and waved his hands in front of him. "No thanks. I think I'm done for the night." He trailed off as if something were wrong.

"Is everything alright?" Jenna asked.

"I don't know. I just started to feel funny," he said slowly.

"What's the matter?"

"I'm not sure. I just don't feel right. Not bad, necessarily, just different. Weird." He said.

"Why don't you go lie down?" She suggested.

"That's not a bad idea," he said, looking completely befuddled. He stood up and instantly became dizzy. Once he stood and looked down, he quickly brought his hands down in front of himself. He turned and struggled to walk into the house.

"Let me help you," Jenna offered, putting her arm around him.

"No thanks, I think I'm okay."

She followed shortly behind him anyways. She walked past the bedroom and slowly started taking off her wine-stained top. By this point, the shirt had dried and stiffened. Jenna couldn't help but smile as she took it off.

She walked into the bedroom wearing her damp bathing suit. "Sorry, I decided to throw the shirt in the washer, but I don't have anything else to wear," she said in a pouty voice. "I hope you don't mind."

Blaine swallowed hard, "No, not at all."

She came over and sat on the bed. "How are you feeling?" She asked, placing her warm hand on his forehead to see if he had a temperature. "You feel fine," she responded. She then put her hand over his heart. "But your heart is beating a mile a minute. You poor thing."

Blaine bit his lower lip. "I'll be fine. I think I just need to sleep it off."

"You're probably right. Is there anything I can get you?"

"No, I'll be fine. You can help yourself to one of Abra's shirts while you wait for your shirt to finish drying. I'm sure she won't mind, as long as you bring it back." He thought about what he said for a minute. "Actually, if you could bring it back before she gets back, that would probably be best."

"Yeah, you're probably right. The last thing we would want is to give her something to be suspicious about. And to find out that you've been drinking." Blaine's breathing was growing heavier. "Exactly."

She got really close to him. "I could put on her shirt, and then bring it back first thing in the morning, but Blaine, do you *really* want me to put a shirt on? I get the impression you like me dressed the way I am." She grabbed the cover and pulled it down swiftly, revealing just how much he enjoyed her lack of wardrobe. He immediately grabbed for the cover, but Jenna grabbed his hand and stopped him. She leaned over him, her breasts now inches away from his face. She put her lips up to his and whispered, "It's okay.

There's nothing to be embarrassed about." She ran her fingernails lightly down his side, tickling his ribs and making him squirm. This just egged Jenna on.

Blaine could feel his heart pounding in his chest. His breathing grew heavier and heavier. All of a sudden, he couldn't control himself anymore. It was as if something exploded inside of him. He grabbed Jenna and pulled her onto him, kissing her hard on the mouth. Jenna put her hands around his neck and kissed him furiously. She brought her head back. Blaine kissed her neck, then moved down her throat. He reached behind her and untied her bikini top, her breasts bursting out. She swung her leg over his body and straddled him. She reached down and unzipped his pants and pulled them down to his ankles. He was still kissing her and moving his hands all over her body. She stopped and stared down at him. All of him. She couldn't believe this was actually happening. She had been imagining this night for years. Sure, she had wished she hadn't had to drug him to get him into bed with her, but once again, desperate times. She always got what she wanted, no matter what it took, and she wanted Blaine Ryan. She got lost in the moment and forgot where she was until he grabbed her around the waist and pulled her on top of him.

Chapter 14

Jenna snapped awake at the sound of the dryer
buzzing that it was finished. She rubbed the sleep from
her eyes. She didn't even remember getting up in the
middle of the night to move the shirt from the washer to
the dryer. She rolled over, but Blaine was gone. She
peaked out the door around the corner. He was in the
kitchen, feeding Norah and Ellie their breakfast. She
turned around and went in the closet to grab the closest
shirt she could find to throw on and walked out. "Good
morning," she said dreamily.

He wouldn't make eye contact with her.
"Morning," he responded flatly. She looked down and
bit her lip. "Your shirt is done in the dryer. I think it
would be best if you got changed and left."

"Blaine, I'm really sorry for what happened last
night," she said. What was one more lie? She thought to
herself. She was neck-deep in them already.

"No. I'm sorry," he said dryly. Jenna imagined
how he was going to finish that statement: 'Sorry you

ever stepped foot in this house. Sorry I ever trusted you with my daughters.' She was completely taken off guard when he continued. "I have absolutely no idea what got into me last night. I am so ashamed of myself. I should never have let that happen."

Jenna slowly sat down beside him. Now she was confused. He was actually apologizing for coming onto her? She couldn't believe it. She realized he was waiting for a response. "Uhh, yeah, you're right. You're married...MARRIED!" She said the word with more anger than she had anticipated. "Well, what should we do?" She asked.

"Jenna, I would be lying if I said I wasn't attracted to you. I mean, look at yourself. You're gorgeous." Jenna beamed from ear to ear.

"But...Abra is my wife. She is the most beautiful woman I know. I love her more than life itself. She's the most amazing woman I've ever met, and she's the mother of my children." Jenna's face quickly turned dark. "I don't know what to do, but I do know one thing. If Abra ever found this out, I would be out the door like that," he said, snapping his fingers. Please promise me she will *never* find out about this. It should never have happened, and I'll be damned sure it won't happen again."

"Abra's a very lucky woman. I guess I'll just get my shirt and be going," Jenna said softly and headed towards the dryer. She grabbed her shirt and held it close to her. It felt so warm against her ice cold body as she walked back to the room to gather her belongings and leave.

Jenna left Blaine's house and went directly for the one thing that might brighten up her morning: coffee. Blaine's house. That's what it was in Jenna's eyes. Not Abra's, and certainly not Blaine *and* Abra's. It was just Blaine's. The love of her life, her soul mate. Even if he didn't realize it yet, he would soon enough. One way or another, Blaine Ryan was going to realize he had made a huge mistake when he married Abra--a mistake that would cost Abra her life, if that's what it came down to. What a shame, Jenna thought. She almost liked Abra. She seemed like a nice-enough person, but nobody was going to stand in the way of her getting what she wanted: not Abra and certainly not Abra's twit of a sister. Jenna finally realized it was her turn to order after the third time the barista asked some variation of, "How can I help you?"

"I just need a small black coffee," she responded.

The barista--Jenna would be shocked if she was old enough to drive a car, let alone serve hot beverages--cocked her head to the side, and stared at Jenna like she was speaking a different language. "Ohh! You mean a tall?" As if Jenna were the idiot for not conversing in this young girl's "native tongue."

No one should be this perky this early in the morning, Jenna thought. "I meant small. As in the smallest cup you have," she snapped back. The girl stalked off. When she came back, she tossed the coffee on the counter, causing some of it to slosh out of the top. Jenna grabbed the cup and held it up in front of her. She eyed it up and down and said, "Just like you, this doesn't look very tall to me." The girl pretended to ignore Jenna by looking around her, asking if she could help the next person in line.

Jenna drove to Nags Head woods, lit a cigarette, and walked the trail as she sipped on her coffee. She knew she shouldn't smoke, but she picked up the habit when she started dieting, and it was a hard habit to kick. This place always amazed her. When someone thinks about the Outer Banks, they think of beautiful beaches, not a forest. Jenna needed to blow off some steam and this was the place to do it. She should be over-the-moon; after all, she got what she wanted. Instead, she was just agitated and annoyed. Was it because she had forced a man to have an affair? *No, that couldn't be it,* she concluded. By the end of her walk, things had become crystal clear. The reason she was so upset was, even though she finally got what she wanted, it wasn't enough. She could not base the rest of her life's happiness on one night. She didn't want him for just one night. She wanted him for the rest of her life. She wanted him more than anything in the world. Her life would not be complete without him. There was only one solution. She had to eliminate the competition, and that's exactly what she planned to do.

Blaine was cleaning up the dishes from breakfast when he heard his cell phone start playing, "I Honestly Love You": his and Abra's song.

"Blaine." Abra said simply.

"What's wrong, Babe?"

"It's my dad. He passed away in his sleep last night."

"Oh, Abra, I'm so sorry. What can I do?"

"There's nothing you can do. I just wanted to let you know."

"Do you want me and the girls to fly up?"

"No, no, I don't want the girls exposed to this. They're going to cremate him and have a short service tomorrow. I would like to stay. What do you think?"

"You should. Don't worry about anything. I have everything under control at home."

"You're amazing," she said,

"Oh no, I'm not, believe me."

"What do you mean?"

"Nothing. I'll talk to you soon. Let me know if you need anything. I love you, Abra. You mean the world to me." He hung up the phone and felt lower than scum. How could he have done that to her? What had gotten into him? He wondered. He never should have gotten drunk. He knew it was a mistake. He hadn't had more than a glass. It shouldn't have had that strong of an affect on him. He started to think about Charlie. The speeches he had given him, including the one at the poker night about loyalty and marriage. He had ruined everything. How could he live with himself after what he had done. He called Abra right back.

"I was thinking, how do you feel about having my mom or Ana watching the girls?"

"Why? What's wrong with Jenna? The girls love her, plus Ana has her hands full, and I would hate to burden your mother like that. Is something wrong?"

Blaine paused. "Of course not. It's just...weren't you upset about Jenna and the girls becoming too close?"

"Well, yeah, but that's not going to change no matter who's watching our girls. I miss them like crazy, and I don't want them to become closer to someone else. If your mom or Ana watches them, she'll be the one who's with them the majority of the time."

Blaine thought a minute. "What about her hitting on me?"

Abra placed her hand on her hip. "My, my, aren't you conceited."

Blaine rolled his eyes.

Abra was growing more confused. "What's going on? Did something happen with you and Jenna?"

"No, of course not. You said you were having a hard time with it. I was just trying to help. I don't want you to feel uncomfortable."

"I'm fine, really, but if you have an issue?"

"No, I guess it's fine."

"I'm sorry, but I can't really think about Jenna right now. I'm just so emotionally drained. We'll talk about it when I get home. I really need to go. We have a lot to get done. Love you! Bye!"

"Love you, too," he said quietly and hung up.

Family and friends traveled from all over to pay their respects to Aaron. As her aunts, uncles, Sadie, and Leah all shared wonderful and hilarious stories about her father, Abra realized she didn't know her father at all. She felt like a complete stranger standing with her family. After not being around her family for so long, she was tired of the subtle reminders that she was the outcast of the family. She was ready to go home to her husband and daughters.

It was finally time for Abra to head back home. Sadie drove her to the airport. The closest airport was Norfolk International Airport, which was a couple of hours out from the Outer Banks, but it was better than the twelve hour drive otherwise.

It had been a long, bittersweet couple of days. Abra had such mixed emotions about what happened. She should be happy. Years of being shunned and disowned by her father. All the yelling and fighting that had gone on had finally come to an end. Her father was finally starting to come around. They were just starting to get along. But she couldn't be happy about any of that because now she had to mourn his death. It just wasn't fair. She was finally happy with her life. The only thing that was missing was her family. She couldn't believe he was ripped away from her again. At least she had Sadie and her mom. She was so happy to have them in her life again.

Chapter 15

Abra was extremely excited to get back to her normal routine and back to her family. Blaine and the girls surprised her at the airport. They brought flowers and a large WELCOME HOME sign that Ellie drew all over. Blaine had assisted Norah and Ellie in covering their hands in paint and covering the sign in her and Norah's handprints. As soon as Abra spotted her family when she stepped off the plane, she ran full force towards them. After she hugged and kissed Blaine and the girls, she noticed the flowers and the sign. "Thank you so much! What a beautiful sign. Did you do this Ellie?" Ellie nodded with a big grin on her face. "You did such a great job!" Abra held on to the girls while Blaine went to search for Abra's luggage on the conveyor belt.

It had been about three weeks since the most memorable night of Jenna's life. Jenna was leaning over her bathroom counter, staring at the little stick....waiting. Who would have thought three minutes could take so long. While she waited she started pondering how she would handle the situation. So far her plan was working perfectly. He would have to leave Abra if Jenna was having his baby. Eventually, the little sign showed up. She gasped.

Abra finally had free time to catch up on some housework. Jenna had been a huge help, but Abra refused to let Jenna do the laundry, which seemed to be piling up, creating a cushiony version of Mount Everest.

"Blaine, can you grab the sheets from our bed?" Abra hollered.

"Sure, be right down!" Blaine called back. Just then, Blaine's phone rang, startling him.

"Blaine, it's Jenna."

Blaine cut her off right then. "Jenna, I don't think it's a good idea if we talk. If it weren't for the fact that I would have to confess to Abra what happened, you would no longer be watching my daughters."

Blaine could hear Jenna sniffling through the phone.

"I really need to talk to you."

"No, Jenna! What happened was a mistake. I don't know how I can get that through your head."

"Blaine!" She said, crying. "I'm pregnant!"

There was a long pause. "Blaine? You there? Did you hear me?"

"Yeah, I heard you. Are you sure?"

"I took a pregnancy test this morning."

"You just took one test? You haven't been to a Doctor or anything?" Blaine's voice began to perk up.

"No, but I just know I am. I've been nauseated, and I'm a week late. I've never been late. Can you meet me at Sam & Omie's?"

"I'm on my way, Blaine said, and dropped the phone. He sat back in his chair, and put his face in his hands. What was he going to do? He had completely screwed up. There was no way of avoiding it. He would have to tell Abra what happened.

"Blaine! I'm putting the laundry in! Can you please bring down those sheets?"

Blaine grabbed the sheets and shook them off the bed. He heard a distant rattle. Sitting along the wall was a small bottle. He walked over and picked it up and read what it was. He stuffed the bottle in his pocket and ran down the stairs.

"Where are those sheets?" Abra asked as he passed by her.

"Sorry, Baby, there's an emergency at the station.. I'll be back soon," he called out to her and ran out the door.

He walked in the door of Sam & Omie's. Jenna was already there waiting for him. She waved him over enthusiastically. He scooted in the booth across from her. "Interesting meeting choice," he commented.

"One of my mother's--if you could call her that--boyfriends loved this place. He was a fisherman. He would come here every morning before he would go out on his boat. I was eight years old. Not quite old enough to stay home by myself. My mom always chose her boyfriends over me, so every morning she would wake me up really early in the morning and drag me here. She just had to have breakfast with him. I would usually just fall asleep in the booth."

Blaine shook his head. "That's all very interesting, Jenna, but that's not why I'm here. Blaine reached into his pocket and slammed the pill bottle on the table. "What are these?"

Jenna swallowed hard. "I have no idea. I've never seen those before." She reached out to grab them, but Blaine pulled them out of her way. Her face turned sour. "Where did you find those?" she said, giving up her act.

"Under my bed, where you dropped them!"

"I can explain," Jenna began.

"There's nothing to explain. You drugged me to get me into bed. Now you're pregnant. I don't think that's too difficult to comprehend."

"So...what should we do about our little situation?" Jenna asked, looking down at her stomach.

"I think we should wait to see if you're actually pregnant."

Jenna grew defensive. "You don't believe me. You think I'm making this whole thing up!" She said.

"No, it's not that at all. I just think one pregnancy test isn't enough to know for sure. Jenna, do you have any idea how much I have to lose in all of this?"

"I am not going to raise this baby alone, so you better figure something out. Either you tell your wife, or I will." She sat back in her chair and crossed her arms. "Hmm...where should I begin? How about, 'Abra, your husband got drunk and forced himself on me?'" She tapped her finger on her lips and cocked her head to the side as if she were in deep concentration.

"No, it would go more like this, 'Jenna drugged me and threw herself at me!'" He shouted, a little louder than anticipated. He looked around and noticed everyone got real quiet and was staring at him. He lowered his head.

"Which story do you think she's more likely to believe? You said so yourself; you don't have the best of reputations when it comes to handling your drinking."

"I'm begging you. Let me talk to my wife about this." Blaine knew that if he could just get Jenna to let him talk to Abra first, he could make his wife understand. If he could just stall it until she went to the doctor's first. There was no point in Abra finding out any of this if Jenna wasn't actually pregnant. He hated keeping a secret like this from his wife. He had never kept anything from Abra. This time, he didn't see any alternative. He loved Abra and his daughters more than anything. If Abra found out that he slept with Jenna, it would be the end of their marriage and their happy little family. Abra would most likely divorce him and take Ellie and Norah away from him.

Meanwhile, Abra picked up the scattered clothes in the bedroom. She noticed a small pile of clothes sitting by Blaine's night stand. She bent over to pick it up and noticed something under the bed. She picked it up and held it up in front of her. It was a hot-pink laced piece of lingerie. She knew for a fact it wasn't hers. That tiny number wouldn't fit around one of her legs. Abra's face instantly turned to the color of Ellie's brick red crayon. She allowed herself to fall limply backwards on the bed. A million thoughts were running through her head. She couldn't believe Blaine would have an affair. Who did the lingerie belong to? What would happen to their marriage and their girls? Should she confront him? Were they going to get a divorce? Would they have joint custody of the girls? How did that even work? She had heard horror stories of men running off with their kids' nanny. She thought about Jenna. She started to blame herself for hiring such an attractive nanny. Up until now she thought they had the perfect marriage. Never in a million years did she think she would have to go through this. She thought about all the women she had pitied in the past for the same exact thing. She would run into them at a party or on the street and feel sorry for them, giving a sympathetic tilting of the head as she asked, "How are things going?" She would now be the one that people pitied and talked about behind her back.

An hour later, Abra heard a car pull up. She jumped to her feet when she heard the car door slam shut. "Where were you?" she asked.

"Sorry I had to run out like that. I wish I could tell you about it, but you know, patient confidentiality." The lie came out quick and unrehearsed. Blaine was even surprised at how easily he was able to lie to his wife. At least he bought himself a little time to figure things out.

"I'm not buying that line. Wanna try again? How about the truth this time?"

Blaine's mouth dropped. How did she know? He didn't know how to respond. He was already in too deep, so he decided to stick with his story. "No, it's true. The lies just came seeping through his pores.

Abra had never been so angry. She could not take one more lie. Blaine looked at her like he had just witnessed Dr. Jekyll turning into Mr. Hyde. Things were fine between them when he left. What had happened when he was gone? Had Jenna called Abra?

"I found this under the bed. Lord knows it's not mine, so whose is it?" She said in an accusing tone, throwing it at him. Blaine caught it.

"I've never seen this before in my life," Blaine defended himself. He was holding the lingerie out by his thumb and pointer finger with a repulsed look on his face.

"Blaine, I want to know whose this is and why it was in our room right now!"

Blaine couldn't remember if Jenna had left them there that night or not. He could hardly remember what happened, but he swore he would have noticed something like that lying around.

"I can't believe you would even think that I would cheat on you! How could you think that? After all we've been through and all this time, you still don't know me or how I feel about you at all!"

"What exactly should I think when I find someone else's panties in our room?"

Blaine didn't know how to respond. He shook his head and stormed out of the room. Abra was flabbergasted. How did she end up being the bad guy when Blaine was the one committing adultery?

Abra heard Blaine's car start up and peal out of their drive. She grabbed the picture frame off of the nightstand and threw it against the wall. The frame shattered. Broken shells and glass covered the floor. Quickly realizing what she did, she fell to the floor, trying to pick the pieces back up and put it back together.

Once Blaine pulled out of the driveway, he drove down the road a couple of miles. He pulled into a nearby parking lot and just sat in his car, completely lost. He needed a plan. He considered going to his brothers, but didn't want to disrupt his wife and kids. They had enough going on in their lives. He thought of the only person he knew who would understand and would be there for him. Sam. Sure, Sam had issues with commitment, but he had always been there for Blaine when he needed him. During one of their fire calls the building was starting to come down. Blaine became light headed and faint while they were inside. Sam grabbed him and drug him out of the burning building shortly before it collapsed.

Blaine knocked on his door. Sam answered the door in *Family Guy* themed pajama pants and a T-Shirt.

"Blaine? What are you doing here?" Sam could tell right away something was wrong.

"Can I come in?"

"Sure," Sam said, stepping aside.

"You want a beer or something?"

"That would be great. Thanks"

"Go grab a seat, I'll be right in."

Blaine didn't say anything, he just walked slowly into the living room and plopped down on the sofa.

Sam came in a minute later and sat down on the sofa beside Blaine and gave him a beer.

"So what's going on? You look terrible"

Blaine explained what had happened. "I think Abra's going to take the girls and leave me."

Sam took a swig of beer, shaking his head. "What the hell happened?"

"Something happened with Jenna when Abra was away," Blaine started.

"What do you mean? You slept with her?" Blaine looked down, ashamed. "I'm not judging, but what were you thinking? How could you do that to Abra? There has got to be something you can do to make this right. You just have to."

Blaine was taken aback by his response. Trying to make light of the situation, he said, "Maybe I'll be like you and sleep with different women every week."

Sam softened his voice. "You know, I've never told you this before, but you have been my inspiration." Blaine laughed out loud. "I'm serious, man."

"Inspiration for what? Avoiding commitment?"

Sam shook his head. "Have you ever thought about why I sleep around so much?"

Blaine chuckled. "To be honest with you, I've never given it a lot of thought. I assume it's because you're terrified to commit."

Sam stuck out his chest. "I'm not scared of anything. The truth is, I'm jealous of you. I go through a lot of women because I'm searching for what you've already found." Blaine had no idea Sam felt this way. "People spend their whole lives looking for what you and Abra have." Sam jammed his finger in Blaine's chest. "Don't screw it up!" Blaine sat there in silence. "Now, I'd be lying if I said there weren't any perks to my lifestyle," he laughed. Blaine thought long and hard about what Sam had said. "Why would you want to be like me? Do you know how miserable it is to wake up alone every morning? Calling people daily on the phone to make dinner plans, just so you don't have to eat alone? The bachelor life isn't as great as you might think. The grass isn't always greener on the other side, man. Talk to Abra and work it out."

"I dunno, man. I really screwed up. I think I should give her a couple of days to calm down. Could I stay with you."

"You can stay here as long as you need, but at some point you're going to have to get this worked out."

Blaine knew Sam was right, but he wasn't ready to face Abra yet. They both needed some time apart.

After Blaine left, Abra grabbed her cell phone and called Sadie. "Sadie, where are you?" Abra said, without so much as a hello.

"I'm at home. Why, what's up?"

"I need you. I just found underwear in our bedroom, and it isn't mine!"

"I'll be on the next flight out," Sadie responded, concerned.

"What about work? You can't make another trip out here."

"Don't worry about it. I have some vacation days saved up that I need to use."

"Thanks. I really appreciate it."

A couple of hours later, there was a knock on the door. "Hey..." Sadie said, emphatically. Abra's eyes were red and swollen. She was squeezing a tissue in her fist so tightly her knuckles were white.

She led Abra up to the living room and walked her over to the sofa.

"Tell me exactly what happened," Sadie demanded, putting a pot of hot water on the stove. She grabbed two mugs, opened the canister on the counter, and pulled out two tea bags.

"I was doing laundry, and I found this under the bed," Abra said and pulled the lingerie out of her pocket and waved it in the air like a flag. "I confronted him, and he ran out. I know it's not mine! Who else could it belong to?"

Sadie shook her head. "I just don't believe it. I know I don't know him all that well, but I never pegged Blaine as the cheating type. He's obviously head-over-heels in love with you and his daughters. I just don't buy it." She paused. "However, I don't trust that nanny any further than I can throw her."

Abra appreciated Sadie trying to make her feel better, but no matter what she said, the evidence was right there in her hands. Abra waved the underwear in the air again. "Obviously, things aren't always what they seem!" She snapped back.

Sadie nodded. She believed this, but she couldn't fight this feeling telling her things weren't what they seemed, but not with reference to Blaine and Abra's relationship. She also couldn't shake the feeling that Jenna had something to do with this. She had seen the way Jenna had been looking at Blaine. She didn't believe they were having an affair, but she wouldn't put it past Jenna to sabotage Blaine and Abra's marriage. She thought back to that night at dinner and how she was drooling all over Blaine like he was a piece of meat. It was obvious to her that Jenna liked Blaine.

Chapter 16

It had been almost a week, and Abra and Blaine were still not speaking except to update on the girls. It was killing Abra. In all the years that they'd been together, they had never gone this long without talking. It was hardest at night after she put Norah and Ellie to bed. This was when Abra felt the loneliest because that was usually Blaine and Abra's alone time together. They would snuggle on the couch and watch a movie, play games, or just be able to have an adult conversation without being interrupted. But for the past week, the only time he talked to her was to check on Ellie and Norah. With everything going on, they both managed to remember what was most important, and that was taking care of the girls and being the best parents they could be.

Abra kept finding herself reaching for her phone to call him without thinking about it. She wanted so badly for things to go back to the way they were, but she wasn't ready to give in yet. Even though it was only

9pm, she decided to go lie down. She changed into her nightclothes and climbed into bed. She turned on the TV and channel surfed. Ironically, it was the night for chick flicks. With every change of the channel, Abra felt worse. She finally came to a channel that was showing *Saw*. Somehow, this movie disturbed her the least. She set the remote on the nightstand beside the bed. As she did, her engagement ring caught her attention. She held her hand up in front of her. Her Princess cut diamond that once sparkled so much it was blinding now seemed like a dull heirloom. The harder she looked at the ring, the more she realized how, without its sentimental value, it could just as well have been from a vending machine. She debated whether or not she should take it off, but realized it was a little too soon to do that. It wasn't like they were divorced, or even separated for that matter. They were just having a fight. All couples fought. She compromised by twisting her diamond so that it was facing down so she couldn't see it. Even though it might not sparkle as much as it did when Blaine first placed it on her finger, it was still too blinding to let her sleep. She pulled her blanket up to her neck, curled into a ball. When she pulled the blanket up to her face, she caught a whiff of an oddly familiar scent but couldn't figure out whose it was. She rolled over and cried herself to sleep.

An hour after she had finally fallen asleep, she woke with a jolt gasping for air. She had to figure out whose perfume that was. Sadie had been staying over ever since Abra called her that night a week ago. She was able to take a couple of days off and told her boss there was a family emergency.

The next morning, Sadie walked past Abra and she could smell that same flowery fragrance. Abra froze. No way did Sadie and Blaine sleep together. Sadie hadn't even been in the same state at the time. That just couldn't be. All of a sudden it hit her. How could she have been so stupid?

Sadie was tired of seeing Abra miserable. She decided to confront the little home wrecker when she came over in the morning. "Hey, Sadie, how's it going?"

"Where's Abra?"

"What? No pleasantries?" Sadie crossed her arms over her chest.

"She's out back making a new picture frame out of seashells." A crooked, sinister smile crossed her face. "Apparently, she broke the other one."

Sadie stared her down.

"Look, Jenna, I know my sister is too nice and too naive to see what's going on here, but I'm not."

"I have no idea what you're talking about, Sadie," Jenna innocently responded.

"I know there's something going on, and all I'm gonna say is that you better back off my sister's husband. They are one of the happiest, most in-love couples I've ever seen, and just because you watch their kids doesn't give you free access to everything in their house." She put her hand on her hip, "Or anyone in it."

"Sadie, I still have no idea what you mean," Jenna said, batting her eyelashes. Sadie turned to walk away. Apparently, there was no getting through to her. "But Sadie, how would you know they're in love. From what I hear, you didn't even attend their wedding. In fact, you haven't even spoken to your sister in years."

Sadie was beyond pissed. "How dare you! You don't know anything about my family or my relationship with my sister!" Sadie was right in Jenna's face at this point.

"Oh, on the contrary, Sadie, I know way more about you than you think. You see, I have been spending a lot of time around here. Abra and I have become close, and she's told me all kinds of stories about you." Jenna put her hand up to her face and scratched her chin. "Actually, I was the reason she contacted you in the first place. What a mistake that was!"

Just then, Abra called in from outside, "Jenna! Can you grab me a paper towel, I made a mess out here. Sure! Be right out!" She turned back to Sadie, "Sorry, Abra *needs* me. Plus, I don't think she wants to talk to you anyway. She recognized your perfume on her sheets." She grabbed a hand full of paper towels and rushed out the door.

Sadie ran after her. "Abra, can I talk to you alone for a minute?" Sadie asked.

"Oh, hi, Sadie. I guess so," she said, but her tone was unconvincing. Jenna tried to get as close as she could so she could hear.

"I want you to know that I have never been in your bedroom when you weren't around. If you smelled my perfume, that's only because that sadistic nanny has the same scent! You have to believe me. I would never do anything like that to you."

Abra was silent for a long time. "I have a lot to figure out and a lot to think about right now. I think you better go, and I'm going to ask Jenna to leave as well until I decide how I feel about everything." Sadie nodded in agreement. Abra stood at the door with her arms crossed as Sadie and Jenna both left.

The pure rage that Abra had felt towards Blaine and whoever the lingerie belonged to had subsided and was now replaced by memories of her and Blaine's life together. She remembered all the good times they had in the past, and it made her feel very depressed to see how quickly her life had gone downhill. She had given up her own family for him. With this thought, as quickly as the anger had dissipated, it had reappeared ten fold. She felt so stupid for choosing him over her family. Maybe her family was right, and she shouldn't have rushed into her marriage.

She was reminded of the famous quote, "It is better to have loved and lost than never to have loved at all." She had always had the strong opinion that anyone who had loved and lost had just wasted time on Mr. Wrong. Now that she was in the position she was in, she couldn't help but have done a complete 180 degrees on this belief. Her mind was flooded with wonderful memories of the two of them and their family. No matter what happened between the two of them she would not consider their time together wasted. She always had and always would believe that Blaine was the love of her life. They'd had an amazing life together thus far, and had two beautiful daughters that Abra felt were and would always remain her greatest accomplishment.

She grabbed a cold glass of iced tea and walked out on the back porch on the lower deck. She laid down in the hammock and stared out across the raging ocean. It amazed her how the ocean and she seemed to share moods. She watched as the waves roared and crashed against the shore, the waves going five feet high before curling over and crashing down hard. The clouds above were dark gray and swirling around. All she wanted was to be able to see the sunset, but looking out, she didn't think the clouds were ever going to clear.

Abra got so caught up in daydreaming about her perfect past, that she completely forgot she had to leave for kickboxing. She hadn't been back since Blaine received that mysterious call. She was overjoyed she had kickboxing that night. She always felt bad about not going back, and since everything started between her and Blaine, she definitely needed to blow off some steam, and she couldn't think of a better way to do so.

"Abra! Over here!" Someone called from across the gym. Abra scanned the room and found Sandy and Maria. She waved and headed over to them. "We've missed you!" Maria said.

"You have no idea how glad I am to be here tonight!"

Just then a dance remix of a song from the 90's started blaring on the stereo. The instructor started shouting out warm-up exercises. Abra jumped in line with Sandy and Maria, creating a grapevine with her legs to the right, clapping at the end, then moving to the left.

The instructor then announced they would start their punching and kicking series. "Jab, cross, hook, uppercut!" the instructor hollered out orders.

Abra closed her eyes and even though part of her felt guilty for it, she pictured Blaine and this woman she didn't even know. This made her think. How could she have such strong feelings against someone when she didn't even know her name? Why was she more angry at this woman than Blaine? The only explanation she could come up with was the fact that her husband

and the father of her children, the man that she knew and loved, would never do that to her.

The kickboxing class was extremely crowded that night and was continuing to swell as late-comers trickled in. It was so packed, Abra wasn't able to fully extend her legs to do her kicks. She became very distracted about the whole situation with Blaine. Who was he with? How long had it been going on? "Back kick! Pretend you're kicking the door closed behind you!" the instructor hollered. Abra kicked with all her might. She was so distracted by her destructive thoughts that she didn't realize how close she was standing to the lady behind her, and kicked her fully in the stomach. The lady screamed and bent over holding her abdomen. Abra rushed over to help her up.

"I'm so sorry!" Abra said repetitively as she grabbed the lady's arm and helped her to her feet.

"What was *that* all about?" Sandy asked as they toweled off at the end of class.

"I'm a little preoccupied with stuff at home," Abra said, chugging down her bottled water. Sandy just stood there, waiting for Abra to elaborate, but Abra didn't want anyone else involved. Minus kicking the other woman, Abra had the best workout she could remember.

Chapter 17

Blaine was walking to his car after a long day at work. He pushed the button on his keychain and waited for the locks to pop up on the inside. He got in, and just as he was about to start the car, he noticed something on his windshield. He reached out his window and grabbed it. It was a piece of paper. He opened it up. It was a note that read, "I'm so sorry. Meet me at Tale of the Whale at 6 for dinner. Just the two of us. Love, Me." Abra and Blaine had not gone out for dinner, just the two of them, since Norah was born, and Tale of The Whale was their favorite restaurant. Blaine breathed a sigh of relief. The fight was finally over and she was going to apologize. He just knew if they had the time to cool off, everything would work out. He didn't leave because of her. Abra didn't do anything wrong. She was completely accurate in her accusation. He left because he just couldn't face her. He wasn't ready to tell her his secret yet. He missed Abra and the girls terribly and couldn't wait to get home. Luckily, he had to dress up for work today, because he was running late and wouldn't have time to go home and change. He forgot his cell phone on the table that morning, so he wouldn't be able to call Abra to tell her he was going to be late. He stopped abruptly at a red light. He reached in his glove box and pulled out his Calvin Klein cologne that he had tossed in there. It also happened to be Abra's favorite. He dreamed of his family and crab cakes as he rushed down Virginia Dare Trail.

Blaine pulled in the parking lot. He looked around, but didn't see Abra's car. He assumed she hadn't arrived yet. He shrugged his shoulders and went in to see if there was a long wait. The restaurant was currently working on landscaping out front. There were shovels and plants tossed haphazardly along the front edge. Blaine walked up to the hostess stand. Standing there was an excessively peppy teenager in a white dress shirt and tie.

"Welcome to Tale of the Whale. How many in your party tonight?" She asked enthusiastically.

"There will be two. It will be under the name Ryan."

"Oh, Mr. Ryan, it looks like your wife is already here. I'll show you to your table," she offered. The energetic hostess guided Blaine through the crowded restaurant.

When the hostess finally stopped in front of a table, it was empty. "This is your table," she gestured.

Blaine looked down at his watch. *Oh no!* He thought to himself. He was 25 minutes late. If he had his cell phone, he could have called to let her know he wasn't going to make it on time. She probably sat there thinking he had stood her up. She probably got pissed and took off.

Just then, the waitress looked out the window towards the gazebo. "Looks like your wife decided to take a walk down to the gazebo." Blaine went to thank her, but she was already gone. He headed out the door towards the deck that led to the gazebo. Blaine scanned the crowd. The deck was scattered with various couples enjoying a night out, but there was no sign of Abra.

When Blaine reached the gazebo, he noticed a lady standing at the far end of the gazebo alone. She had her back to Blaine and was looking out at the water as it softly crashed at the base of the gazebo. Blaine had no idea what was going on, but he was starting to get a really bad feeling. The lady must have sensed someone approaching because just then she turned around, her red hair whipping in the wind. A huge mischievous grin painted on her face. She briskly made herself over and embraced Blaine in a strangling hug that lasted so long Blaine gasped for air.

"Mmm, you smell really good," she whispered in his ear.

Jenna took his hand and encouraged him to sit down on the benches that encompassed the perimeter of the gazebo. She was wearing a long slinky emerald green dress which really emphasized her blood red hair and green eyes.

"Jenna, what do you want?" he said, frustrated with himself for not seeing this coming earlier.

She leaned her elbows on the rail and leaned back looking at the sky. "I've been waiting for you for nearly ten years," she said.

Blaine was taken aback. "What are you talking about?"

"Sarah told me that it was just a charity case, but I knew differently. I knew that you really loved me."

"Sarah? Sarah who?"

"Sarah Wrigley. My best friend in high school."

The gazebo had cleared out by this time, and it was just Blaine and Jenna standing alone. Sarah Wrigley. The moment Jenna mentioned her name, he had a strange feeling of déjà vu. If Blaine remembered correctly, she was a freshman when Blaine was a senior. She was always hanging out with an overweight girl his friends were always making fun of and bullying. It all came rushing back like he had been hit by a wave. He finally knew why Jenna looked so familiar that first day when they had her over for dinner. After he graduated, he had heard she was admitted to the psychiatric ward.

"Laney? Is that really you?" he said, completely overwhelmed by everything that was going on.

"Laney. Blah! I haven't been Laney in years. She's gone. I'm Jenna now. You know this."

"Look, I'm still not sure what's going on here, but I want you to stay away from my family," Blaine ordered. "I thought I made it perfectly clear to you that I am madly in love with my wife. I love my family more than anything."

She took a step closer. She was standing so close now, Blaine could smell her mint breath, and it gave him shivers down his spine. He moved back, but she fell right into step.

"Your lips are saying one thing," Jenna said, placing her manicured pointer finger on Blaine's lips, "but your eyes say something completely different."

Jenna gradually moved her finger down his lips, snaking her finger down his neck, down over his heart, down his stomach to his navel. When she eventually reached the top of his pant line, Blaine grabbed her hand and pushed it back at her.

"Goodbye, Laney." He turned to walk away.

"What about our baby?" she called out to him.

"I don't care what you want to do, but I don't want anything to do with you anymore."

As he stormed out of the restaurant, he went to grab for his cell phone and then remembered he had forgotten it. He had his hand on the car door handle when he heard a loud cracking sound and then everything went black.

Jenna stood over his limp, unconscious body holding a brick she found by the building in hand. She looked down and something caught her eye. She bent down to pick it up. Blaine's knife had fallen out of his pocket. She smiled and tossed it on the passenger seat. She struggled to drag Blaine's noodle-like body into the back of her car. "I'm so sorry, Baby. Someday you will understand and thank me. You will see that this is how it's supposed to be." She closed the rear hatch and sped down the road.

Blaine woke up feeling completely discombobulated. He had lost track of time. How long had he been out for? Fifteen minutes? An hour? He looked around, there was nothing even remotely familiar to him. He tried to bring his hand up to soothe his pounding head, but he couldn't. His arms were stretched out above his head and were bound to two bedposts. He glanced down. His legs were also bound, and he was sprawled out on a bed. They were starting to cut off his circulation. He could feel blood trickling down the back of his neck. It gave him the chills. He took a deep breath and was nauseated by the iron smell of the blood. The last thing he remembered he was talking to his children's nanny. Next thing he knew he was tied to a bed looking like the Vitruvian man.

Jenna walked in, wearing a thong and a see-through laced nighty. "Jenna, what are you doing?"

"You don't understand, Blaine. I ALWAYS get what I want." She climbed on top of him. "And I...want...you," she said, tapping him on the nose.

"Jenna, what part of 'not interested' don't you understand?"

"You were interested when your wife was out of town."

"You drugged me and took advantage of me."

"Oh, like you didn't like it," Jenna snapped back.

"Jenna, I'm a married man. I love my wife, and I thought I made that perfectly clear. It's against the law to keep me here against my will!"

"Oh Baby, this is nothing compared to what I have planned for your precious wife."

Blaine's heart jumped. "What did you do to Abra?" he asked, terrified. He thrashed back and forth, trying to get out of the ropes.

"Let's just say she won't be bothering us anymore." She stroked his cheek, and he whipped his head to the other side.

"If you so much as touch a hair on her head, so help me!" Blaine yelled back.

Jenna, ignoring his comment, finally pretended to notice his injured head. "You poor thing! I'm going to get a rag to clean you up." She walked out of the room.

He immediately looked around for an exit strategy. He couldn't find one. He was trapped, and she had complete control over him. There was only one thing he could do. He took a deep breath and prayed Abra could forgive him.

Jenna came back with a bowl of hot soapy water and a rag. She set the bowl on the table beside the bed. She grabbed the rag and rung it out tight. She unravelled it and started blotching at his head.

He took a deep breath and looked her in the eyes. "Thank you," he said as sincerely as he could.

"You're welcome. I'm here to take care of you." She smiled.

"I don't mean for cleaning up my wounds. I mean for knocking some sense into me." Jenna gave him a perplexed look. Clearly not what she had been expecting. "Ever since that night, I haven't been able to get you out of my mind." Blaine swallowed hard. "I love you, Jenna," the words tasted bitter in his mouth.

"I love you too!" she said, quickly. An automatic response to what she had been waiting her whole life to hear. Jenna was getting ready to say something and then stopped. "Wait," she looked down at her stomach. "You only love me because I'm carrying your baby. You wouldn't want anything to do with me if it weren't for that fact."

"That's not true. I love the fact that you're carrying my baby, but that's not the reason I love you."

"You really mean it?"

"Of course."

Jenna bit her lip. "In that case, I have something I need to tell you." Blaine raised an eyebrow. "I…" she trailed off.

"What is it Jenna? Just tell me!" It came out harsher then he had anticipated, but his wife's life was on the line. That was, of course, if she was still alive.

Jenna didn't seem to notice the edginess in his tone. She pulled hard on her shirt and started twisting it. "I may not be pregnant after all."

"What are you talking about?"

"I wanted you to love me. I thought I was, but I was wrong. I knew the only way you would leave Abra and be with me was if I was having your baby, but now you say you'll love me whether I'm having your baby or not, so I thought I should come clean."

Blaine was relieved, but he tried not to let it show. He had to get untied and out of this house. He had to find his wife and daughters. He thought about what he should say next. "Oh Jenna. You must have been feeling pretty desperate to think the only way I could ever love you was if you were carrying my child." Blaine nodded toward the mirror on the other side of the room. "Look in that mirror. What do you see? I'll tell you what I see. I see a beautiful, intelligent woman, who's not afraid of anything."

"No, you don't really mean that." Jenna said, turning away from the mirror.

"I would hug you, but I'm a little 'tied up' right now." This time he cringed at his own joke.

Jenna thought it was the funniest thing she had ever heard. She threw her head back and laughed manically.

Blaine opened his eyes wide, thinking, *you insane woman.*

She threw her hands up. "Of course!" she said, shaking her head. She rushed over and untied him. He hugged her, waiting just the appropriate amount of time, and in one swift motion he flipped her onto the bed, took the rope, and worked on tying her hands to the bed. She wriggled free. Now she was pissed. She grabbed the pan of water and hit him in the face, water exploding all over the room. He fell backwards on the bed. Jenna stormed out of the house.

Abra came home from work to a quiet and empty house. Sadie said she would take the girls out for the day and give Abra a little time to herself. Abra didn't realize when she agreed just how lonely she would be. The silence was a painful reminder that Blaine still hadn't returned. He came over the previous night to see Norah and Ellie, but things were too tense so he ended up leaving shortly after.

Abra had to have picked up her cell phone a million times and started to dial his number before she came to her senses and quickly hung up. She paced back and forth like a nervous lioness in a cage at the zoo. After twenty minutes of imprinting the carpet from pacing the same path, she was finally ready to give in and give up. She was going to call and apologize and give Blaine the chance to explain his side of the story.

Her fingers were shaky and unsteady as she fumbled with the phone, trying to dial. The pounding of her heart was so strong she could feel it thumping in her ears. Once the call finally connected, she could faintly hear something buzzing in the distance. She looked

over and saw the newspaper moving on the coffee table.
She slowly walked over to the table and picked up the
paper. It was Blaine's phone lighting up and shaking
wildly on the coffee table. Of course he would forget
his phone! She had always trusted Blaine whole-
heartedly, but there was a small feeling inside her that
kept egging her on, and that feeling was hot-pink and
lacy. Never had she even crossed the line by snooping
in his e-mail or checking his phone. Now, however, the
only thing holding her back was the fear of what she
might find.

She picked up the phone and rolled it over and
over between her palms. Her fingers gently caressed the
buttons as if it were a detonator to an explosive. She
slowly went into the text inbox and scrolled down
searching for numbers she didn't recognize. Most of
them were from Abra, with a few from guys at work
and his brother. Part of her was relieved, but she was so
full of guilt that she couldn't enjoy it. She went through
the discarded messages and the sent mail but didn't find
anything out of the ordinary. Abra was almost
disappointed that she didn't find anything. At least it
would have helped her to figure out whose panties she
found under her bed. What did it matter? They weren't

hers and that's all she cared about. She caught another whiff of the perfume, and it all became clear. Then she knew exactly what she needed to do. Something that should have been done a long time ago, which she forced herself to believe wasn't right in front of her. She picked up her phone and made a call.

When Jenna arrived at the house, she slowly walked in. She unwrapped her scarf, took off her hat and coat and laid them in a pile on the sofa. "Abra? Anyone home?" She called out. It was eerily quiet. She crept up the three flights of stairs to the kitchen. When she got to the top, Abra was at the table in the dark. Her mascara streaked down her face.

"Jenna, please sit down." Abra was shaking inside--partially with fury and partially nerves. She couldn't believe she was in this situation, let alone having to confront her husband's mistress now. "Jenna, I know something's been going on between you and Blaine. I hope you understand that I can't have you watching my daughters, and I can't have you in my house anymore."

Jenna looked down, trying to hide the fire in her eyes. "I see. I'm sorry. I don't know what to say. I guess Blaine told you everything then?"

Abra paused. "No, not exactly. All of the clues pointed to you." Jenna didn't say anything. Abra's phone started ringing. Abra stepped away from the table.

"Hi Sadie," Jenna heard as Abra walked away from the table. Jenna looked around. Abra was still on the phone. Jenna quickly reached into her purse and pulled out a bottle. She poured the powder in Abra's drink that had been sitting on the table. She swirled it around and watched as the powder dissolved.

Shortly after, Abra returned. "Jenna, I trusted you with my daughters. I thought you and I were friends, and yet this is how you treat me? You sleep with my husband! I can't even stand to look at your face right now."

Jenna hadn't one clue what Abra was saying. Her eyes were fixated on Abra's drink. She was growing very impatient. Finally, Abra finished speaking and took a sip. She swished it around in her mouth before swallowing. She had a strange, suspicious look on her face. A couple minutes later she stood up and sat back down quickly.

"Something wrong, friend?" Jenna asked sarcastically.

Abra shot her a suspicious look. "I'm not feeling good right now." Abra stared at Jenna, then looked down at her drink. "Jenna. What did you do?" She gasped as she faded out of consciousness. Jenna watched as Abra's body went limp and slid off of the chair and onto the floor. Jenna grabbed a rope from the back of her car and tied Abra's arms and legs together and dragged her heavy body down the stairs. She tossed Abra's body in the back of her car like she was a sack of grain, slammed the door shut and rubbed her hands together. *Now that that's taken care of*, she said to herself, and hopped in the Tahoe and drove off.

Blaine finally regained consciousness. He slowly set himself up in the bed. He quickly made his way through the halls. He looked around and saw picture frames on every table and across the mantel. As he walked past, he did a double take. "What the hell?" he said as he picked the picture up. The picture was familiar. It was their family photo for Christmas cards, but where Abra was supposed to be was Jenna's smiling face. He continued looking around the house. There were pictures all over the place. All of which either had Abra's face cut out and replaced with Jenna's, or they were of Jenna, Ellie, and Norah. He saw something sitting on her dining room table. It was a book. He went over to get a closer look. It was a scrapbook. He quickly flipped through the pages, watching his life through the years flash before his eyes. Pictures and articles from his high school football games, graduation, his wedding, and the two births of his daughters. He looked at the final page. On the page adjacent to the Nanny Advertisement that Abra had put in the newspaper was a hand-written piece of paper. It was taped with scotch tape at the four corners. In big red letters it read, MAN LOSES WIFE IN FALL FROM CURRITUCK LIGHTHOUSE. Blaine was baffled and terrified. This woman was obviously unstable and dangerous and after what she had done to him, there was no knowing what she was capable of. He ran out the door, but soon realized he was stuck. He didn't have a car. He had no way of getting to his wife.

He ran back inside and looked for a phone, but couldn't find one.

He ran back outside. Just then, a lady pulled in the driveway next door. She jumped out of the car and ran in the house, leaving the car running. Blaine waited until she went inside and jumped in the car. The lady ran back out screaming.

"I'll bring it right back, I promise! It's an emergency!" The lady chased him down the road.

He flew into their driveway. He left the car running, jumped out, and ran into the house, leaving the car door hanging open. "Abra!" he shouted, running through the house. He ran up and down the stairs, still shouting her name. Once he reached the top, he bent over, holding his side as he tried to catch his breath. There was no sound. There was no sign of Abra or his daughters anywhere. What did that monster do with them? He had a moment of panic. Blaine thought back and remembered that Abra had told him in the minute conversation they held earlier that Sadie was taking the girls to the Aquarium that day. He wondered if Abra had told Jenna where the girls were. He looked at his watch. It was 4pm. He knew the Aquarium closed at 5. Hopefully, they were still there.

He sped down Airport Road and flew into the parking lot. He jumped out of the car, slammed the door, and ran towards the building. He had almost reached the building when he heard screaming coming from behind him. He turned around and saw a young woman whip her arm out and point towards the ticket booth. Blaine rolled his eyes. He didn't have time for this. His wife's life was on the line. He ran back to the ticket booth, reaching for his wallet along the way.

"What can I do for you, sir?" She asked in a pleasant tone, as if she hadn't just yelled at him.

He threw a $10 at her. "Keep the change!" he hollered back as he ran towards the building again. He almost ran straight into a giant shark mandible on display. He ran past the Rattlesnakes and an enormous plastic frog. He looked high and low for Sadie, but couldn't find her. He ran through the otters and turtles, when it hit him where they would be. He ran as fast as he could to the Close Encounters exhibit. There his daughters were. Sadie was holding Ellie up and over the tank so she could touch a sting-ray. Norah was in the stroller next to her. At least his daughters were safe.

"Sadie!" Blaine yelled.

Sadie jumped, almost dropping Ellie in the water. "Blaine? What's going on? Is something wrong?"

"Abra's in trouble. Jenna took her. I don't have time to explain. We just need to go!"

"Come on girls," Sadie said, trying not to cause a scene or create panic.

"I'll drive," Blaine said as they ran out the door.

"I never liked her! I always knew there was something weird about her!" Despite everything going on, Blaine found that last comment amusing and chuckled. Sadie took out her cell and called 911.

Chapter 18

Jenna was so proud of herself. Sure, she would have liked to tie Abra to the top of Cape Hatteras, the tallest lighthouse in the country, but this was a lot closer. Carrying a woman up 214 steps was exhausting. There were platforms after every so many stairs with information about the history of the lighthouse. Jenna stopped on each platform to catch her breath, but she had to move quickly or else Abra might wake up. She walked to the center and looked up the spiral staircase. Not too much further now.

She was dragging Abra across the final platform when Abra started to stir and regained consciousness. When she finally realized what was happening, she started screaming and kicking at Jenna's hands. Jenna lost her grip, and Abra scrambled on the ground, struggling to get to her feet. Abra kicked her as hard as she could, sending Jenna flying towards the spiral railing in the middle. Jenna fell back against the railing, almost falling over the edge. Jenna growled and darted towards Abra. Abra moved quickly at the last second, sending Jenna straight into the wall. Jenna turned around and went at her again. Abra tried to move, but just as she did, Jenna grabbed her and threw her towards the railing. Abra tried to stop herself before she went over the railing, but she wasn't fast enough. She slammed straight into it, sending her over the edge. Abra quickly grabbed the metal rail before being sent to her doom. She shut her eyes, trying not to look down. She struggled to get her grip and pull herself up and back over. Once she was back on the platform she rushed towards the steps. All of a sudden, something hit her in the back of the head. She saw stars, her vision got blurry, and then she blacked out.

Jenna picked Abra's lifeless body up again and continued dragging her the rest of the way up. She looked at the small window on the platform, then squeezed through the small door. She took out the rope she had and tied Abra to the railings. She took one final look at Abra. "You shouldn't have gotten in the way," she said in a matter of fact tone. Just then there was a huge crash of lightning and it started pouring rain. Jenna turned around and headed back down the staircase.

Abra woke up with the worst migraine she had ever experienced. Her vision was blurry, and she was disoriented. When she was finally able to see, she wished she would pass out again. Her hands were bound to some sort of railing. She wiggled her body towards it. She pushed her body up against the railing and looked through the frigid, black, metal bars. Once her eyes focused and she realized what was on the other side of those bars she instantly started hyperventilating. She trashed around, screaming, trying to escape from the ropes. She had to be 15 stories high. The last thing she remembered before she lost consciousness again was the sound of footsteps and a flash of light.

Abra had a quick flashback of all the times Blaine would talk about all of the lighthouses and how badly he wanted to take her, Ellie, and Norah up to the top of each one to look out. Blaine loved the thought of standing high above the trees, looking out across the Atlantic Ocean. Nothing sounded more terrifying to Abra. Anytime he would mention it, a cold chill would travel down Abra's spine. Now, here she was, tied up on top of one. Her arms bound tightly to the rail so she had no choice but to look out. She shut her eyes again, but it didn't help. Even with her eyes shut, she knew what was out there, almost as if her eyelids were transparent. She screamed, but there was no one there to hear her. When she thought about her daughters, she let out a blood curdling scream that sounded like something from a horror movie. Where were they? Were they safe? She got a horrific feeling in her stomach. She had told Jenna that Sadie was taking the girls to the aquarium that day. She frantically attempted to get untied, but whenever she moved, the ropes tightened on her wrists almost to the point of cutting off circulation. This was a tourist attraction. Maybe there were tourists down at the bottom. She wiggled herself closer to the railing and slowly forced herself to look down over the edge. Her heart started racing, and she started to sweat, making her even colder. She had no idea how long she'd been stuck up at the top. She wondered if Blaine was worried about her. If he even knew she was gone.

Jenna was halfway back down the stairs when she heard screaming. She ran back up. She forgot to gag her. Abra had dirt on her face. Her hair was soaking wet. She was shaking.

"Jenna, why would you do this to me?" Abra stuttered.

"Look Abra, Blaine and I are supposed to be together. That was the plan. That's always been the plan. You just got in the way. No one gets in the way of what I want." Jenna was towering over her. Jenna pulled out Blaine's knife from the bag she had been carrying. Abra's heart was pounding. She swallowed hard. There was nothing she could do to protect herself from this maniac.

"Jenna, please. Think about my girls!"

"Ellie and Norah will be well taken care of; don't you worry. You are replaceable, Abra. Those girls are still young enough that in a couple of years, I'll be the only mom they'll remember." Jenna raised the knife and brought it down towards Abra's small, helpless body. Abra ducked her head down and slid her hands up as high as she could. The knife came down, slashing through the rope, freeing Abra's hands. Abra jumped up and ran towards the exit. Jenna let out a scream of frustration. She had just reached the door when Jenna grabbed her legs, causing Abra to fall, landing with a loud thud. Abra started kicking and screaming as Jenna grabbed a hold of her in a tight grip and pushed her up against the railing. Abra's hands were so wet and shaky she couldn't get a good grip on anything. She finally stood up. This fight wasn't over. Abra trusted Jenna with her family, and all the while she was plotting to phase her out. It surprised Abra how much animosity she could have towards one person. The anger started brewing and boiling up inside of her.

"Nobody messes with my family!" she said through gritted teeth as she came towards Jenna, poking her in the arm with each word. "You need to back off and leave us alone!" She gave Jenna one last poke.

Jenna started pushing back, forcing Abra to the edge. She stood up straight, towering over Abra. "You ruined everything! Blaine and I were meant to be together! From that day he stood up for me in high school and got those horrible, horrible guys away from me, I knew he loved me. Then here you come into the picture and take everything away. Blaine and I were supposed to get married. Those should be my girls! You took my life from me!" With each accusation Jenna took a large step towards Abra, eventually backing her against the wall. "Do you know how hard it is to be nice and kiss up to your enemy? Cooking, cleaning, and being all sympathetic like a true friend when you're so over-the-top jealous of everything she has it makes you wanna throw up?"

At this point, Jenna and Abra's noses were touching. Abra was completely lost. *High school? Blaine and Jenna knew each other?* This was all too much for Abra to handle. She took the palm of her hand and brought it up quickly, jamming it up to Jenna's chin. Jenna's head snapped back. Abra knocked Jenna to the ground and ran for the door. Jenna fell right beside the knife. She grabbed it and jumped back up, coming back with a vengeance. She grabbed Abra's arm just as she had almost reached the door and slammed her against the lighthouse. Her head cracked against the hard cement. Right away, Abra saw stars. She struggled with Jenna, trying to get the knife off of her. It flew out of Jenna's hands and over the railing. They both looked down over the edge in horror. Jenna picked Abra up and tried to lift her over the edge. Abra kicked Jenna as hard as she could in the stomach. Jenna dropped her and grabbed her stomach. Abra hit the ground, landing on her right shoulder. She could hear something pop, but she jumped up as quickly as she could. Abra tried to bring up her right arm, but the pain was too excruciating. She took her left hand, grabbed Jenna by the neck and brought it down at full force, smashing Jenna's head into Abra's knee. Jenna fell to the ground, unconscious. Abra ran through the door and blocked it from the inside with a big stick that had been laying there. She rushed down the steps, gasping for air, looking over her shoulder every couple of steps. Every step she took caused a shooting pain up her right arm. She cradled it as best as she could.

Blaine and Sadie flew through town with a trail of cops and an ambulance behind them. They hoped and prayed they weren't too late. They made a sharp turn in the parking lot, and the police cars and ambulance quickly came to a halt, surrounding the Tahoe. The policemen jumped out of their cars and barreled towards the lighthouse.

Blaine threw open the car door and ran behind the cops. Abra stepped out from the lighthouse only to be surrounded by officers with their guns pointed at her. Blaine ran in front, "STOP! Don't shoot!" He ran over and grabbed Abra in a huge hug, almost suffocating her. Both had tears in their eyes.

"Where's Laney?"

"Who?"

"Jenna! Where's Jenna?"

"Up at the top." The group of cops ran inside the lighthouse. Sadie ran up to her and grabbed her in a tight hug.

"I already lost you once. I couldn't handle it again."

"Where are the girls?" Abra asked. She couldn't hide the fear in her voice.

Sadie pointed towards the car.

They walked up to the car and looked in on their two beautiful daughters, Ellie was kicking her feet and Norah was playing with a toy.

Blaine put his arm around Abra. She looked up at him and kissed him sweetly. Blaine bumped Abra's arm, causing Abra to scream in pain.

"What's wrong?" Blaine asked.

"I think I dislocated my shoulder."

"Sadie, will you stay with the girls a minute?" She nodded and jumped in the car to keep the girls company. Blaine lead Abra over to the ambulance.

"Let me look at it," he told her, rolling up her shirt sleeve.

Abra instantly screamed, then relaxed, "Ahh," she said in relief as her shoulder popped back into place. Blaine hopped up in the ambulance. He grabbed a sling and helped Abra put her arm into it. "That ought to make you more comfortable until we get home," Blaine said as they got into their car with Sadie and the girls.

"Hold on a second! We have a lot of questions for you!" one of the policemen yelled after them.

"Do we have to do that now? I think my wife's been through enough in one day," Blaine asked.

"I guess we'll probably have our hands full with the redhead for tonight," the officer responded. "But stay close to home!" he added.

Abra smiled because she couldn't think of anywhere else she would rather be. They got in their car and breathed a sigh of relief. Blaine started driving as they all sat in silence.

"How about I interview nanny's next time?" Blaine joked, trying to break the silence.

"Deal," Abra agreed.

"I actually wanted to talk to you about that," Sadie jumped in. "I talked to my boss the other day and I might be able to get transferred to the area...but I would need a place to stay?" she said slowly. "I could help watch the girls."

Blaine and Abra looked at each other. "I guess we do need a new nanny," Abra said lightly as she turned to Blaine. "It's ok with me, but do you think we should do a background check?" Blaine responded with a smile. Abra and Sadie smiled at one another knowing that they would finally have the chance to become the sisters they wanted to be.

As they got closer to home Abra looked at Blaine and wondered how things could ever be the same again, but she knew there was no one else she would rather have by her side. She turned around to see Ellie and Norah, fast asleep. As she watched them in adoration, she envied their innocence to the cruelty of the world and promised herself she would never let anyone hurt her family again.

HILLARY CRAIG

Is a graduate of Kent State University. Her love of writing began when she was assigned to write her first poetry book in middle school. Since then she has written poetry, short stories, and her first novel, "A Dream Come True" was published in 2004. She currently lives in Columbus, Ohio with her husband, Andrew.